TOMBSTONE

Wyatt Earp—By law, by fear, by violence, he ruled Tombstone.

Doc Holliday—No one was fooled by his racking cough and mysterious ways. He was still the deadliest man in Tombstone.

Dan Stockard—He arrived in Tombstone undercover but quickly got swept into the town's bloody secrets.

Nellie Cashman—She was the miners' angel and swore she would bow to no man though she found herself falling in love with the mysterious Dan Stockard.

The Stagecoach Series
Ask your bookseller for the books you have missed

STAGECOACH STATION 4
TOMBSTONE

Hank Mitchum

Created by the producers of
**Wagons West, White Indian,
Saga of the Southwest,** and
The Kent Family Chronicles Series.

Executive Producer: Lyle Kenyon Engel

BANTAM BOOKS
TORONTO · NEW YORK · LONDON · SYDNEY

TOMBSTONE

A Bantam Book / published by arrangement with
Book Creations Inc.

Bantam edition / February 1983

Produced by Book Creations Inc.
Executive Producer: Lyle Kenyon Engel.

ISBN 0-553-20717-2

Published simultaneously in the United States and Canada

PRINTED IN THE UNITED STATES OF AMERICA

O   0 9 8 7 6 5 4 3

Author's Note

Tombstone is a work of fiction; however, most of the characters it describes existed, and the incidents actually occurred.

A full century has passed, and today the motives and circumstances surrounding the bloody events of October 26, 1881, are shrouded in legend and controversy. This book tries to sort out the facts and make a plausible guess or two as to what really happened that day, and why.

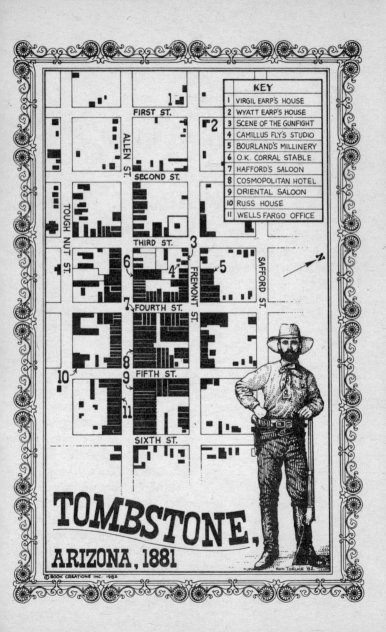

KEY

1	VIRGIL EARP'S HOUSE
2	WYATT EARP'S HOUSE
3	SCENE OF THE GUNFIGHT
4	CAMILLUS FLY'S STUDIO
5	BOURLAND'S MILLINERY
6	O.K. CORRAL STABLE
7	HAFFORD'S SALOON
8	COSMOPOLITAN HOTEL
9	ORIENTAL SALOON
10	RUSS HOUSE
11	WELLS FARGO OFFICE

TOMBSTONE,
ARIZONA, 1881

Chapter 1

Dan Stockard was having a late breakfast at a table where he could watch the activity on the main street of Benson, Arizona. Even when he saw the stagecoach come tooling up before the railroad depot, he continued to take his time. Having finished his coffee, he rose and got his wide-brimmed hat from the seat of the chair beside him. A methodical person, he adjusted his coat, easing the hang of it to conceal the shoulder holster beneath his left arm. He put on the hat and stepped from the restaurant into a sunlit morning in October 1881.

Up the street, in front of the station, the stage horses were stomping restively. Express packages and luggage, including Stockard's leather suitcase, were being stowed in the boot and lifted onto the top rack, and passengers from the station were starting to load. Stockard, approaching, sized them up. Judging from appearance, one of the men was a stockman. Another, better dressed, might be a prosperous silver-mine operator on his way back to Tombstone, accompanied by his wife. A third looked like a minor courthouse official or perhaps a storekeeper. Two plainly dressed, middle-aged women appeared to be traveling together.

The driver made his appearance. He was a whip-lean

fellow with sunburned features and a yellow handlebar mustache that framed his mouth, its untrimmed horns stained by the chewing tobacco tucked into one leathery cheek. He carried a mail sack that, like his passengers, was being transferred off the Southern Pacific train from Tucson, fifty miles to the west. Having tossed the canvas sack into the forward boot, he stepped up on the wheel hub a moment to stow it safely there. He cocked a glance at Stockard, who called up, "Anybody scheduled to ride on the box with you?"

Before answering, the driver took in the tailored coat, the white shirt and cravat, the waistcoat with silver watch chain looped across the front. His critical gaze considered the face beneath the hat's wide brim—the dark hair, worn a trifle long, the clean-shaven features that might be a shade too sharp for a woman to call handsome. The man shrugged. "We're carrying no shotgun this trip. If you've bought a ticket, you can ride where you like."

"Thanks," Stockard said, and easily swung himself to the box.

By now, the rest of the passengers had taken their places. After a last check of his teams, the driver climbed to his seat, sorted out the reins, and laced them expertly between fingers that were as tough as the leather itself. He kicked off the brake.

"All right, you crowbaits!" he hollered in a voice that picked up the ears of the horses—four wiry, muscular animals with the look of mustangs. "Let's get outa here!"

The crack of the reins was as effective as any whiplash. As one, the teams leaped into their collars. The coach rocked on its thoroughbraces, almost forcefully enough to snap Stockard's head upon his neck if he hadn't been prepared for it. Like a shot, they were off down the rutted street, a film of dust quickly screening the iron gleam of the railroad they left behind.

Frame and adobe buildings of the town fell back. Soon they were in the open, and having made a dramatic exit, the whip brought his teams in and settled them to an easier pace. The stagecoach rolled south, following the course of a murky yellow stream Stockard judged to be the San Pedro River.

He resigned himself to a lengthy ride, the broad brim of his hat tilted to protect his face from the high smash of sunlight. From his breast pocket, he took a flat cigar case, selected a smoke for himself, and offered the driver one. The latter eyed the cigars but shook his head. "I like to eat mine," he said around the bulge of tobacco distending one cheek. Stockard returned the case, dug up a match, and shielded the flame between his palms as he got the cigar burning. Smoke whipped away in the wind of their passage.

They took the ungraded roadway to the sound of wheels spinning on their axles, the creak of timbers and leather, and a steady hoofbeat rhythm. The valley of the San Pedro stretched before them in air so clear the mountains at either hand seemed like two-dimensional backdrops on which the eye could follow the course of every dry ravine and crease and stratum in dun and gray. The surrounding land was stippled with the thin green of desert grass that looked hardly enough to support the cattle ranches that occupied much of this region.

Overtaking a big freight rig, also moving south, they were briefly swallowed in the fog of yellow dust trailing its massive wheels. As the dust thinned and was blown away, Stockard commented, "A dry country!"

The other man considered the statement. "That could depend," he said finally. "Where you from?"

"San Francisco, most recently."

"Well, then, I can see you might notice some difference. It's no lie that hereabouts a man has to prime himself to work up a good spit!'' Whereupon he leaned and loosed a brown glob over the side of the boot.

Stockard had questions he would have liked to ask, but he had an idea the driver would clam up if he thought he was being pressured. He propped a boot against the framework of the coach and made himself comfortable, working at his cigar in silence.

He was aware of the driver studying him from time to time with sidelong glances. He kept his silence, and presently the man's own curiosity got the better of him. ''Your first time in Tombstone?''

His passenger gave only a brief nod in answer.

The strategy worked. After several more minutes, the other man picked up the broken thread of their talk himself. ''It may be we're dry,'' he conceded as though there had been no pause in conversation, ''but we're lively. Two years old and already the biggest town in Arizona Territory. I know of fourteen different faro layouts working both day and night. I don't mind a look at the cards myself, from time to time. And I can tell you . . . the Alhambra, the Oriental, the Crystal Palace—whatever your action is, you won't have any trouble finding it.''

So he's taken me for a gambler, Dan Stockard thought, and was satisfied to let it go without correcting him.

Presently, the stage road took a crossing of the river at a ford that was so shallow, in this gaunt season, that it barely wet the hubs of the big spoked wheels. On the opposite side, the passengers alighted to stretch their legs, walking up and down beside the coach while the teams were allowed to drink. Later, as they resumed their journey through the dry growth along the San Pedro's east bank, Stockard wanted to know, ''How much farther we got to go?''

"Fifteen, twenty miles. We'll be in Tombstone toward sundown, barring accidents."

"Such as a holdup?"

That got him a sharp look. "You been hearing stories, I guess. But hell! They don't waste time on us when we're making the run this direction. They want us going *out*—bringing out bullion."

"You been held up?"

"Personally, you mean?" The man shook his head sharply left to right. "Ain't had the honor yet. But I only been driving hereabouts for something less'n a month. Time I first hit this country, I figured I'd quit staging awhile and maybe try my hand prospecting instead. Well, if there's any silver left to find in those hills around Tombstone, somebody with better luck than me is gonna have to do the looking!

"But now that I'm back to handling the ribbons, I figure it's just a matter of time, particularly on this run between Tombstone and the railroad. This corner of Arizona has got the dandiest bunch of outlaws you ever run into! They hang out at Charleston, bold as brass—that's a mill town, south of here on the river. Up till a couple years ago, when the silver strike was made at Tombstone, they mostly made a living stealing beef from each other and from the Mexicans and running contraband across the border. Now the mines have given them a brand new sideline—robbing the treasure coaches. And they've been doing real good at it."

"Can't the law stop them?" Stockard asked.

The man lifted a bony shoulder. "Sheriff we got here—fellow named Johnny Behan—he ain't no damn good! After every holdup, he sends a posse, but nothing ever comes of it. So Wells Fargo puts a shotgun messenger on any outgoing coach that carries bullion, and hopes for the best. . . ."

Sometime later, as they braked to ease down into a brushy draw, the driver gestured with a handful of leather reins. "Right here," he said, "one of our coaches run into trouble on an evening, back last spring. In March, it was—and it's one time the bastards didn't get what they were after. But it cost a couple of lives. Coach was headed the other way, naturally—for Benson. One story has it there was eighty thousand in silver in the box, which sounds dumb to me because that much weight would likely have busted the axles. More likely she was carrying something like twenty-five thousand, which ain't exactly to be sneezed at, either.

"The driver that night was Bud Philpot, a prince of a feller. He'd had to slow to climb out of the draw, and somebody yelled out of the shadows for him to throw down the box. Not Bud, though! He just whipped up his teams, and when he did, the bastards started shootin'. Three of them—they killed Bud right off, and a passenger who was riding up top—fellow by the name of Pete Roerig. But the gent riding shotgun knew his business. He fired back and then grabbed the reins and kept the horses running, and they left them killers standing there!

"A wire from Benson brought the sheriff and a posse out from Tombstone. That was a little too late, but I guess they did find a feller who gave them the names of the three that done the killing."

"And?"

The man looked at Stockard. "How do you mean, 'and'?"

"Was that the end of it? Didn't the posse bring them in?"

"We're awful close here to the border. They all three made it over, safe. But then, a few weeks ago, we heard a couple had got themselves killed trying to hold up a store over to New Mexico. And not long after that, the third got his, along with Old Man Clanton and part of his outfit, when some Mex'cans they'd been rustling from caught them in an ambush in Skeleton Canyon. That finished the last of the three.''

The driver spat a wad of tobacco, then wiped a sleeve across his mouth.

''Well,'' he went on philosophically, ''outlawing is a tough line of work in this country. There's a lot that don't grow old at it! Still, it does seem that bunch was kind of unlucky when you figure they never even got in smelling distance of the twenty-five thousand—or eighty thousand—or however much it actually was.''

Through the chaparral, perhaps a mile ahead along the San Pedro, Stockard glimpsed an oasis of trees gone brown and ragged with autumn, a small clutter of adobe buildings, a dazzle of sunlight bouncing from windowpanes.

''Drew's Station,'' the other man said. ''We change teams there.''

Dan Stockard wasn't quite ready to drop the subject of the aborted stage job. He chose his words carefully. ''Sounds to me that holdup must have been the same one I heard some talk of back there in Benson. It caught my ear because I thought someone mentioned a name I'm familiar with: John Holliday—the gambler they call 'Doc'. . . .''

The other shot him a wary glance. ''You a friend of Doc Holliday's?''

''I've never actually run into him on the circuit. But I'd heard he was in the neighborhood, along with his friend Wyatt Earp.''

''You heard right. Thanks to all that mining money, a lot of the big-time gamblers have been hanging out in Tombstone—including the Earps, the whole clan of them. Doing pretty good for themselves, I understand.''

''Maybe *too* good, according to the talk I heard,'' Stockard suggested. ''Some kind of rumor that Holliday might have been in on the robbery—that he was the one who shot the driver and the passenger. And that it was Wyatt Earp who set up the job and planned it and then rode out with the sheriff's posse and threw them off the trail. You heard any such talk as that?''

Getting no immediate answer, he glanced at his companion. The driver's jaw, behind the straggling yellow mustache, was bunched hard on the tobacco that filled his cheek; he stared straight ahead at the rumps of his horses. When he spoke, it was to say with chilly emphasis, ''Mister, where Doc Holliday and the Earps are being talked about—for the sake of my health, I make it a point not to hear a damn thing!''

Dan Stockard didn't press him further.

They stopped briefly six miles south of Drew's Station at Contention City, where an ore-reducing mill filled the valley with the steady throbbing of the stone-crushing stamps. There the postmaster removed a handful of letters from the mail sack and added a few items franked for Tombstone. Then they left the river, swinging eastward, with the sun a hard pressure against backs and shoulders as the coach road began the final ten-mile climb out of the valley and toward the barren hills where, three years earlier in 1878, Ed Schieffelin made his fabulous strike. With the traffic that used this stretch of road, especially big ore wagons hauling to the mills, the dust was heavier than ever. Powder dry and hub deep in places, it was raised in choking clouds by horse hooves and the winds that blew the valley's length.

Dan Stockard asked, ''What've the Apache been up to this season?''

The driver—Stockard had heard someone back at Drew's Station call the man Nat Gower—lifted gaunt shoulders in a shrug. ''Things have been fairly quiet. I guess the Chiricahua are kind of restless up there on the San Carlos Reservation, but if they take it in their heads to bust out, they'll probably head for Mexico. They're scared of the army boys over at Fort Huachuca.

"You ask me, this country's got more to worry about just now than Injuns!"

Afternoon dragged on. The mountains grew larger and bolder, the desert growth thicker behind stinging curtains of dust. The trouble, when it came, burst on them without warning.

Three horsemen spurred out of the brush and converged on the coach before anyone could have been aware of them. There was a glint of sunlight on gun metal; voices shouted, muffled behind the cloths pulled up over the riders' faces. One moved to head off the teams. A second rider appeared beside the forward boot of the coach, and the long barrel of his handgun covered both Stockard and the driver, the thing accomplished before either had a chance to move toward a weapon. At the gunman's harsh order, Nat Gower muttered crossly, "Oh, hell!" and tromped on the brake, his steady pull at the reins bringing the team to a halt.

The man holding Stockard and Gower under his gun appeared to be the leader. He gave an order, and the one who had cut off the horses fell back to lend a hand covering those inside the coach. Glittering eyes, shaded by the brim of a shapeless hat, stared at the two on the box. Voice muffled by the mask, the outlaw warned them, "Don't make any mistakes!"

"You've made the mistake!" Gower retorted angrily. "You picked the wrong coach. There's nothing on here you want."

"Not even a payroll?" The bandit indicated Stockard. "Then what the hell's *he* doing?"

"Not riding shotgun if that's how you figure. He's just one of the passengers."

For the first time, the outlaw seemed less than sure of

himself. As he peered narrowly at Dan Stockard, his companions waited, and the passengers inside the coach sat frozen in their places. Finally, the bandit kneed his horse closer so he could glance into the boot of the stage. When he saw there actually was no shotgun there, he swore. But he wasn't through with Stockard. He ordered roughly, "Open your coat."

Stockard slowly spread the wings of his coat front to show he had no gun belt strapped about his waist. But the man had good eyesight. He had caught a glimpse of the holster and gun handle beneath Stockard's left arm. "One of those!" he grunted. "All right—take it out real easy and drop it!"

Stockard was not about to quarrel with a revolver pointed at his head. Using the tips of his fingers, he slid the gun from its holster and let it fall to the ground beside the big front wheel. The bandit looked past him at the driver. "You, too," he ordered. "I can see you got a gun. Get rid of it!" Nat Gower swore at him fiercely but did as he was told, pulling the weapon from his hip holster and pitching it over the side of the coach.

The bandit was looking now at the silver chain looped across the front of Stockard's waistcoat. "What's on the end of that thing—a watch or a rabbit's foot?"

His face a mask, Dan Stockard fished the watch from his pocket. It was a good one, with a silver case, and about the size of, and not much thicker than, a dollar. "Not a rabbit's foot," he remarked coldly.

The man in the mask gave a snort. "It should've been, because this ain't one of your lucky days. I'm in need of a watch. I'll take that one." He snapped his fingers sharply. "Hand it over!"

Inwardly seething, Dan Stockard obeyed and saw watch and chain disappear into a pocket of the bandit's trousers.

"Now—let's have the mailbag," the fellow said, pointing up toward the boot where the canvas sack was stowed away.

That drew a bellow from Nat Gower. "Mister, you know lifting the U.S. mail is serious business!"

"Shut up!" the outlaw snapped back at him. "You got no treasure box, so we'll take what you *do* have!" And he wagged the barrel of his gun at the men.

Stockard was already following orders. He leaned and got hold of the canvas sack and straightened up with it. But in the same motion, he swung the heavy sack in the direction of the bandit—hard! The outlaw saw the danger too late. His yell broke off as the weight of the bulging sack struck him full in the chest and knocked aside the arm that held the gun. His fingers inadvertently crimped the trigger. A shot cracked flatly in the desert stillness, and the frightened horse shied, for a moment out of control.

Almost without thought, Stockard let the sack go and dove over the side of the coach, catching at the rim of the big wheel to break the force of his fall. He struck the ground, went to one knee, and grabbed up the gun he had dropped moments earlier. At the same time, the outlaw managed to get his horse under control so he could try a shot. Two guns spoke together—in their haste, both missed. But they drove the horse close to panic. It tried to bolt, coming around in a dust-raising circle as its rider used a heavy hand on the reins to settle it.

Suddenly, there was complete confusion. Men were shouting. Still another gun went off. Stockard didn't know if it belonged to one of the other bandits or to someone in the stagecoach. A woman screamed. And now, with it all, the team horses began acting up; the coach rocked violently as the cursing driver fought his lines.

Stockard was on his feet, peering through streaking dust as the bandit on the gun-shy horse tried again to target him.

Stockard fired twice in quick succession. The first bullet picked the hat from the outlaw's head, and with the second, his animal got the bit between its teeth. In its scrambling, it almost fell under its rider, and in another moment, it had spun away, both horse and rider disappearing into the dust and the screen of desert growth.

Suddenly, it was all over.

Stockard heard hoofbeats quickly retreating and fading into silence as all three riders scattered, apparently giving the thing up for a bad job. Order began to be restored. The coach horses had been brought under control again. Men came piling out of the vehicle. The rancher still held the smoking gun he had managed to get hold of and fire during the skirmish.

Nat Gower, having quieted his teams, was down from his seat demanding to know if anyone was hurt. Apparently not, though one of the women was weeping in near hysteria while her companion tried to comfort her. Stockard caught sight of the hat he had shot off its owner's head; he picked it up and shook the dust from it. Handing it to the driver, he said, "I don't suppose this tells you anything?"

It was a decrepit piece of headgear, sweat-stained and stiff with grease. Nat Gower examined the thing with a look of distaste and thrust a finger through the hole Stockard's bullet had punched through its crown. "It tells me only the sonofabitch is lucky he still has a top to his skull! Hell, there's a thousand hats just like it floating around the territory— no earthly way to tell any of them apart." In disgust, he flung the battered object away, sending it kiting across the sandy earth.

Stockard retrieved the mail sack and handed it over. Gower took it with a nod of thanks and tossed it up into the forward boot. "All right," he told his passengers. "Let's load up again. Everything's taken care of—thanks to having someone up here on the box with a cool head and no nerves at all! What *is* your name, friend?'' There was new respect in his tone as he looked at the stranger.

Stockard had his lie ready. ''It's Shaw. David Shaw.''

''If you ask me, Wells Fargo could use more men like you to ride herd on these stages. Interested in a job, maybe? I'll be more'n glad to put in a word for you.''

''Well, thanks. But I got other plans.''

''That's too bad. At least I'm glad you were along *this* trip! They spoiled my record, but I guess nobody's any the worse off.''

''Not quite true,'' Dan Stockard said as he turned to climb back to his place. ''I'm out a damn fine watch!''

Chapter 2

Nellie Cashman, on an errand of friendship, had left her rooming house and restaurant at the corner of Tough Nut and Fifth streets and walked the short distance to the edge of the Mexican section. In Tombstone, a layout of streets and buildings spilling off the treeless promontory known as Goose Flats, nothing was farther than a few cramped blocks from anything else. Yet, just two years in existence, this mushrooming place had a population that was already supposed to rival that of the Old Pueblo—Tucson.

Parts of Tombstone weren't supposed to be safe for respectable women, unattended, even in broad daylight. After nightfall, when the camp really let loose, almost none of it was. But Nellie Cashman knew this town well and was not one to be intimidated. She had been on her own and sufficient unto herself much too long for that. She felt perfectly at ease in a place like Tombstone.

There seemed to be no one home in the shack belonging to Virgil Earp and his wife, Alvira. Having knocked and gotten no answer, Nellie Cashman turned and crossed the rutted intersection, at an angle, to another adobe on the northeast corner of Fremont and First. Wyatt and Mattie Earp lived here.

No question about it, these Earp brothers were a clannish outfit, and considering the way they made enemies, it was probably no wonder they crowded their families so tightly together, as though for mutual protection and support. Morgan Earp and his wife, Lou, actually shared Virgil's home, while Jim, the oldest brother, lived right next door with his wife and teenaged daughter; so far, the rest of the clan remained childless.

Nellie herself had no particular liking for any of these men, but then she supposed she could be prejudiced. She did like the Earp women, however, and felt more than a little sorry for them.

At Wyatt's and Mattie's, the door was open, and she heard women's voices. Calling a greeting, she let herself in and went through to the kitchen where Mattie was busy ironing. The open windows did little to dissipate the heat of the wood stove, where a fire burned to keep the irons in readiness. A sad young woman, Mattie Earp, and with good reason to be. Besides Wyatt publicly flaunting his affair with another woman, it was said he had never seen fit to marry Mattie—or so Nellie had heard. In fact, there was reason to doubt any of these Earp men had ever bothered to marry the women they lived with. Watching Mattie now at her labors, flushed cheeks sweating, Nellie Cashman felt a stir of resentment as she thought of the heedless cruelty of some men.

Alvira—Mrs. Virgil Earp—was seated at a crude, oilcloth-covered table with a cup of coffee in front of her. Both women greeted Nellie warmly, and she accepted the invitation to pour herself a cup. "I can only stay a minute," she told Alvira. "I came to bring you a letter."

"A letter?"

"It was picked up with yesterday's mail, in care of the Russ House. But your name is on it."

Nellie handed it over. Alvira Earp took the envelope,

frowning as she said, "But I don't never get no mail!" She was a tiny thing, slightly dish-faced but cute as a button. She had been working as a waitress in a hash house in Nebraska when Virgil Earp—a footloose stage driver at the time, already widowed—first laid eyes on her and decided she was just what he wanted. She struck Nellie Cashman as a little silly but with a good load of feisty spunk packed into her diminutive frame. She turned the envelope over and over. "Well, that's my name, all right." She peered at the postmark. "From Globe—Arizona Territory."

Mattie turned to her. "You don't know nobody in Globe."

Eager now as a child with an unexpected present, Alvira's little hands trembled as she ripped the envelope open, took out a single sheet of foolscap, and unfolded it. Her lips moved as she laboriously made out the penciled writing. "Why," she exclaimed, "it's a letter from Kate!"

"Kate Holliday?" Mattie returned from the stove, where she had gone to get a freshly heated sadiron. "We ain't heard a word from her since she left town so sudden—that must have been three months ago! But what would she be doing up in Globe?"

"Running a boardinghouse," Alvira said, a forefinger marking her place in the letter. "She says she bought into it with five hundred dollars she got out of Doc when they busted up. She says she knew we'd be anxious to know where she is and how she's making out." She gave Nellie a pert nod—there was a suddenness, something almost birdlike, to her every movement. "Thanks a heap for bringin' the letter. I always liked Kate, though I never did figure what she could see in that awful Doc Holliday!"

Mattie, frowning, tested the iron with a moistened finger. "I still don't see why she sent your letter to Nellie Cashman."

"Don't you?" Alvira said dryly.

All at once, there was a stillness in the room. Looking from one woman to the other, Nellie sensed the unspoken tension.

"What are you talking about?" Wyatt Earp's wife demanded.

Alvira drew a breath. "Surely you ain't forgot already about the mess that was stirred up—the reason Kate had to leave Tombstone?"

"You mean the paper she signed? The one tying Doc in with that stage holdup?" Mattie gave a sniff and a toss of the head. "It didn't mean nothing. She said afterward that Sheriff Behan got her drunk. Kate and Doc had one of their rows, and she only signed the thing to get even."

"It was a dumb fool way to do it!" Allie replied. "And she knew it soon as she was sober. Her and Doc always made up after their fights—but not that time. He wasn't gonna forgive being arrested and hauled before the judge and having to prove an alibi! She cleared out of town for her own good, and now she ain't taking chances. Says right here in the letter—" Alvira skimmed the page, pointed at a line with her finger, and read, " 'I'll be sending this to Nellie Cashman so as it don't fall into the wrong hands.' " Then she looked back up at Mattie. "She ain't quite ready yet for Doc to find out where she's gone to. You ask me, I think she's scared to death of him. At least when he's drunk."

"But we wouldn't tell on her," Mattie protested.

"No, *we* wouldn't," Alvira replied with a knowing glance at Nellie.

"Just what do you mean by that?"

Nellie gave her the answer as gently as she could. "Mattie, she means your husband."

The young woman stared at her and then at her sister-in-law. "Wyatt?"

"Oh, Mattie! Wake up!" Alvira's patience had slipped,

as it was all too prone to do. "Don't you know Kate is even more scared of him than she is of Doc? She told me once, it's one of the main things the two of 'em used to fight about—her wanting to get clean out of Tombstone, free of Wyatt. She always claimed he had Doc under his thumb. Doc jumps when Wyatt says *frog*!"

"Oh, that's silly!"

"But it ain't!" Alvira was on her feet, facing up to her sister-in-law. Mattie wasn't very tall, but Virgil Earp's wife looked almost like a child confronting her. "It's plain truth! Wyatt has got him a way of making some folks do anything he wants. What are Virge and me doing in Tombstone? We was getting along fine up at Prescott till Wyatt showed up and talked Virge into trying his luck here. Well, it's been two years now, and how much have any of us got to show for it? But Virge won't leave the place as long as Wyatt's around."

"Kin *should* stick together!" Mattie retorted. "But nothing's holding Doc Holliday against his wishin'. You make it sound like Wyatt was some kind of bogeyman!"

"He's beginning to act like one," Alvira said harshly. "I swear, of late he's so growly and mean I'm near scared of him myself!"

"That's only because he's been under a lot of strain. It's all that talk going around about him planning those stage robberies. . . ."

"How do you know it's only talk?" Alvira asked.

Mattie's head snapped up. *"Don't you go saying that!"*

"Mattie, I honestly can't see why you bother standing up for him! Not after the way he treats you—and the whole town knowing all about it. I tell you, if Virge was to try doing to *me* what Wyatt and that woman, that—that Sadie Marcus . . ."

With concern and growing alarm, Nellie Cashman had been listening to these angry voices and watching Mattie Earp turn white of face and trembling. She was about to interrupt before something worse was said when, all of a sudden, their talk was ended by the slamming of the street door at the front of the house. Her breath caught, and she saw the exchange of glances as they heard a tread of boots approaching.

The tall and solid shape of Wyatt Earp filled the kitchen doorway.

For a moment, no one moved or spoke. From his stern look, it was impossible to know if Wyatt had heard any of their argument. Gray eyes in a narrow face, above a hard trap of a mouth with its generous sweep of tawny mustache, surveyed each of the women, resting longest and with an expression of plain dislike on Nellie Cashman. His mouth curled as he said roughly, with something near to contempt, "You ladies sound like a bunch of hens carrying on!"

If he expected an answer, he didn't wait for it. He looked at Mattie standing beside the ironing board. A basket filled with the clothes she had finished pressing stood on a chair nearby. Wyatt flipped through the stack with the well-manicured fingers of one hand. "You got a clean shirt ready here for me?"

"It ain't ironed yet, Wyatt," his wife replied quickly. "I wasn't expecting you home quite so early. I'll have it done right away, and then I'll put supper on."

He shook his head. "I won't be eating here. I got other plans tonight."

From the way Mattie blanched, her hand shaking so much she had to set down the iron she was holding, it was as if he had struck her in the face. And he might as well have, for this would be another night of seeing him dress up in his best, spurning the meal she had planned to fix him in order to escort his mistress to one of the town's expensive restaurants and return home sometime before morning only if it suited him. Wyatt Earp's complete indifference to the suffering he caused his neglected wife was a thing that roused Nellie's

Irish temper. Yet it was none of her business, and she had to clamp her jaw to keep from saying something that would have done no good at all.

Wyatt seemed unaware of what he had done. He turned away from Mattie's anguished stare, and his eye lit on the sheet of foolscap lying on the table. "Well!" he grunted, "And what's this?" He picked it up.

Belatedly, Virgil's wife reached for the letter, saying, "Gimme that—it's mine."

"Oh? How am I supposed to know that?" When she tried to take the paper, Wyatt tightened his grip, and they stood with it between them, caught in a sudden contest of wills. Tiny as she was—the top of her head barely reaching to his chest—Alvira met his chill look with one of angry defiance.

"It's mine, I said!" she repeated hotly. "And it's personal. Doesn't nohow concern you!"

"I'll decide as to that," Wyatt Earp said. "I won't have anybody keeping secrets from me in my own house. Now let me read this."

"*No!*" She almost screamed it, and she must have taken him by surprise. With all her wiry strength, she suddenly wrested the letter from him, and spinning around, she jerked open the stove and thrust it inside. She looked at Wyatt in angry triumph as the paper curled and blackened and burst into flames.

Nellie thought for a moment he would surely strike her. But he had caught sight of something on the floor, and he turned and swiftly scooped it up. It was the discarded envelope. Not giving Alvira a chance this time to interfere, he warded her off with his shoulder while he glanced at the writing. Slowly, his head lifted, and his stare caught Nellie Cashman.

"So *you've* got something to do with this. 'Care of the

Russ House,' '' he quoted. ''Now I wonder how my brother Virge would enjoy knowing you been acting as a go-between for his wife in some kind of secret correspondence—and who knows what else!''

When she was angry, the brogue Nellie Cashman brought with her from Ireland became broad enough to cut with a knife. She came up from her chair, her hands clenched to hold them steady as she faced the tall man. She could feel her cheeks flaming. ''I suppose I know what you're thinking— but I've done nothing wrong, and so far as I know, neither has Allie. Sure, and neither of us has any reason to be apologizing to *you*, Wyatt Earp!''

His jaw and his mouth were stubborn as he answered with an irritable shrug. ''Oh, I'd know better than to say a word against Nellie Cashman. Not in public, anyway. The town wouldn't hear a word against the woman who nurses its sick and feeds its poor and hungry. But I heard you've taken in that Roerig woman and her kids—and she's one that says I planned the holdup when her husband got shot off the coach. She's called me a murderer, to my face! And how do I know you haven't come here to spy on me—looking for something that would maybe back her claim?''

Wyatt flung down the envelope. ''This gives me a right to tell you to leave my house—and stay out of it!''

Nellie managed to hold her temper as she studied him in silence, trying to gauge the forces at work in this strange man—a man who had arrived in Tombstone trailing vague legends of his prowess as a law officer of some kind in distant Kansas. Since coming here, he'd ridden as a shotgun messenger on Wells Fargo's treasure coaches before serving briefly as a deputy sheriff. Nowadays he dabbled in town lots and mining claims but chiefly made his living running the gambling concession at the Oriental Saloon—and apparently it paid him well. Yet he kept his wife in virtual poverty in this hovel in a squalid corner of Tombstone. Meanwhile, he hobnobbed with the town's political leaders and shamelessly flaunted his affair with the Marcus woman, who was a stage performer and the former mistress of Sheriff John Behan.

Nellie was outwardly calm as she told him, "I can't say that I'm interested in you one way or another, Mister Earp. It doesn't bother me at all if you want to order me out of the house." She took her reticule from the back of the chair and hung it on her arm, and Wyatt Earp stepped aside for her as she crossed the room to the door. Watching, Alvira declared suddenly, "He can't order you away from *our* place—mine and Virge's. You're welcome there any time at all you feel like it."

Nellie smiled her thanks but didn't answer. She was still seething minutes later as she walked along Allen Street, on her way home to the Russ House. She hardly noticed as the afternoon stage from Benson passed her, boiling into town in a thunder of hooves, slam of timbers, and swirl of gritty dust.

The last few miles before Tombstone were a dusty punishment as traffic on the stage road increased. The Benson coach crept past heavily laden ore wagons heading for the mills along the San Pedro on broad wheels that ate deep ruts into the rocky soil. Nat Gower told Stockard that one rig, loaded with much-needed timber for a virtually treeless Tombstone, had hauled all the way from the Huachucas to the southwest—the Dragoons were nearer, but the Apache made logging there too risky a proposition. Just about everything the town used, including a big share of its water, had to be hauled in. It made for steep prices.

More and more there was evidence that they were approaching a place of feverish activity: accumulated trash, the litter of abandoned camps, the remains of workings and test holes that proved worthless and had been quickly abandoned.

In a few places, squalid clots of tents and brush lean-tos had collected into temporary communities that, Stockard learned, prided themselves with such names as "Gouge-em," "Hog-em," and "Stink-em." . . . And, finally, there was Tombstone itself, spilling off its low mesa and, in back, a barren hill that was heaped and scoured with the buildings and workings of a dozen mines, smoke fouling the blue desert sky from a small forest of stacks.

The town, in a first glimpse, looked as barren and featureless as the mesa it stood on. Stockard saw a spread of flat-roofed, mostly one-story buildings, and an instant later it seemed the coach was caught up and surrounded by the place. A stuttering of hammers and screech of saws assaulted them. Hard to believe that none of these structures, whether of adobe or of wood, had been standing three years earlier, before Ed Schieffelin made his strike.

Actually, a good bit of Tombstone was even newer than that, according to Nat Gower. A fire, just this past summer, started in one of the saloons, got out of hand, and destroyed a large section in the very heart of town. But already the gutted buildings had been replaced.

Gower shouted at his teams and sent them leaning into the harness, to go tearing along a main thoroughfare—"Allen Street," he shouted in answer to a question from Stockard— that must have been a generous eighty feet in width. Stockard had an impression of crowded wooden sidewalks, plate glass, false fronts crowded cheek by jowl along the street, and a profusion of painted signs that he had no time to sort out. A block of these . . . two blocks. Then the driver was standing on the brake and bringing his coach to a slamming halt in front of a squat adobe building. Stockard saw a signboard with the painted legend *Wells, Fargo & Company*.

"End of the line, I take it?" A little stiff from the hours

of inactivity, Stockard was glad enough to stretch and prepared to climb down from the high seat.

Wrapping his reins about the brake handle, the driver said, "Normally I haul in at the post office, but they're gonna want to know about what happened. Here comes Marsh Williams now."

"Local agent?"

The driver nodded and turned to climb from his perch, taking the mail sack with him as a precaution. Stockard dropped down the big front wheel, walked around the vehicle, and stepped up on the wooden sidewalk in front of the Wells Fargo building. Amid a babble of talk, passengers were climbing out of the coach.

As he brushed an accumulation of road dust from his clothing, Stockard looked for the man Gower had identified as being in charge. He stood on the doorstep—a man of average size, running a shade toward overweight, with thinning hair and wire-rimmed spectacles. The fellow beside him was younger, thin featured, with an air of scowling discontent. He wore sleeve protectors, and a shock of unruly black hair overhung the beak of a green eyeshade. A clerk, no doubt.

Agent Williams was questioning his driver sharply. "Held up?" he echoed.

"That's what I said," Nat Gower told him. "They jumped us, maybe halfway this side of Contention. Three pistols, with handkerchiefs over their faces—couldn't put a name to any of them."

The Wells Fargo agent looked stunned. "But what in the world were they after?"

"Anything they could get, I reckon. They thought maybe I was carrying a payroll. They sounded plumb put out to learn I wasn't. Instead, I come near to losing the mail sack—only, we happened to be in luck." He peered around, spotted Dan

Stockard, and waved him over. "This here's the one that stopped 'em. Calls himself Dave Shaw."

"Shaw?" The agent gave him a careful look and then a quick smile and the offer of a soft and uncalloused hand. "I'm Marshall Williams. You save the mailbag?"

"It was quick thinking and quick moving," the driver assured him. "You ought to seen it! He traded some bullets with them, and they all three give up and made a run for it. Hell of it is he lost a nice-looking silver watch in the process; but that's all they did make off with."

There was a clamor just then from the stage passengers, who had been waiting around for someone to release their luggage from the rear boot. Williams nudged his clerk and said, "Go help them, Harry."

The young man bridled. "Isn't my job!" he protested. But, with an angry shrug, he went to unstrap the leather shield and hand the passengers their belongings.

Williams turned back to Dan Stockard. "Mind stepping inside a moment where there's less confusion? I'd admire to hear a few more details."

"All right." Stockard followed him into the building, and Nat Gower tagged after, still toting his mail sack over one shoulder.

The Wells, Fargo & Company office, a low-ceiling adobe whose thick walls kept out the worst of summer heat and winter cold, was lacking in elegance. Behind the long counter with its gate, which cut the room in half, were bins for storing packages, a couple of wooden file cabinets, and a bookkeeper's desk and high stool. The open door of the agent's private office, partitioned in one rear corner, showed a desk and chairs and a large, green-painted metal box safe.

Nat Gower was eager to give details, and Stockard let him, interrupting only when the driver started to build up his story in a way he felt was too flattering. The Wells Fargo agent listened with lips pursed, nodding thoughtfully and putting in an occasional question, while his gaze rested appraisingly on the stranger. As this was going on, the door opened, and a newcomer entered. Stockard, seeing the sheriff's badge pinned to his coat, knew who it was before Marshall Williams said, "Here's Johnny Behan."

The sheriff of Cochise County proved to be a dapper, dark-haired fellow in his late thirties, well-groomed, with a carefully trimmed mustache, his slim good looks marred by the fact that he was already on his way to going bald. Stockard remembered the stage driver's unequivocal statement— *He ain't no damn good!*—and at first glance, he was inclined to think Behan would likely be more successful as a politician than as an upholder of the law in a tough land.

The sheriff said, "I heard some noise about a holdup." On being introduced by the Wells Fargo agent, he gave Stockard a politician's smile and handshake and listened attentively as the details were spelled out for him. Afterward, he swore and shook his head, saying, "Well, I suppose I could take a posse out, but it don't sound like it'd really be worth it or would accomplish anything."

At that, Stockard caught Nat Gower's shrug and sour expression, as though to say, "That's no surprise!"

"Looks like it was a freak sort of thing," the sheriff went on, "hitting a stage that obviously couldn't have anything aboard of any value. Usually, they show better judgment than that."

Nat Gower commented dryly, "Could be it's time there was armed guards on *all* the stages. If anyone's in the market, they could do worse than to start looking right here." And he indicated Dan Stockard with the stab of a callused thumb. "You'd have admired to see the way he handled himself. Cool as a cucumber—and not afraid to use a gun, either."

Williams eyed the stranger thoughtfully. "You looking for a job?"

Stockard quickly shook his head. "Not really."

"I know—that's what you said," the driver grunted. "Too bad. I sure wouldn't mind you setting on the box next to *me*." He changed the heft of the mail sack on his shoulder. "Well, I'm running late. Got to take this to the post office and then run my outfit around to the barn."

On his way out, he passed the clerk, who came in still wearing the same sulky expression. Without a word to anyone, Harry went through the gate in the partition and climbed onto his stool to resume work on the office ledger. Shortly afterward, Johnny Behan excused himself, shook hands again with Stockard, and was gone in a cocky swagger.

Marshall Williams turned to Stockard. "I won't keep you any longer, Mister Shaw. If you should change your mind about a job, look me up. I might be able to use you. Meanwhile, Harry Phelps there will help you if you want to put in a claim for that watch you lost."

"Later, maybe."

"Well, anyhow, let me bid you a rousing welcome to Tombstone, Arizona Territory."

And Dan Stockard, with a dry smile, replied, "Thanks, but I think I already had one. . . ."

Chapter 3

A block west of the Wells Fargo office, on the north side of Allen Street, Dan Stockard signed for a room at the Cosmopolitan Hotel. Someone unfamiliar with the ways of frontier mining camps might be surprised to find that this crude adobe building, on a street of jerry-built and graceless structures, was well fitted out with carpeting and hardwood floors and that the small but comfortable rooms should boast of wallpaper and quite adequate furnishings.

Stockard unpacked his bag, stripped off his traveling clothes, and after washing up, used soap and razor on a stubborn crop of beard stubble. Dressed again, he took several papers from a secret compartment of his bag as well as a sizable packet of greenbacks, from which he selected a number, and placed them in his wallet. His gun, with the spent shells replaced, was in its holster. Finally, he got his wide-brimmed hat and left.

After a leisurely meal in the hotel's restaurant, during which he carefully observed the other diners, Stockard stepped out onto the street. The last daylight was fading from the sky, the swift desert dusk already settling, leaving an afterglow along the barren horizon. With it came the early-evening chill—at this altitude in autumn, the contrast between day and night could be extreme. From habit, he fumbled for his watch and shook his head as he realized timepiece and chain were gone. For a moment, he had forgotten they were stolen.

Allen Street was tuning up. The day crews were coming off their shift at the mines, and men from out of town were descending on the area at day's end. Lights were burning in all the saloons and gambling halls, which stood cheek by jowl along the dusty streets of Tombstone's business district. Dan Stockard made his way along the noisy boardwalk, looking through open doors and plate-glass windows, taking a preliminary survey. A knot of riders came tearing in from the west, sombreroed and noisy—in off the dry ranges where cattle outfits were reluctant neighbors to the upstart town and its silver mines. Stockard saw how the newcomers were quickly sized up by the sharp eyes of women parading the sidewalk and by gamblers who loitered in front of the saloons looking for business. It was no place for the gullible.

He left the sights and sounds of Allen Street behind, his own interest lying elsewhere just then. He had been given directions and, though he was a stranger, located the house without difficulty. It stood in what was clearly a residential section for the upper stratum of mining camp society. Though these houses, too, were nothing more than frame and adobe, they sat well apart from one another on separate lots. And even in the dark of full night there was a suggestion of affluence—of the wealth being dug out of the shouldering hills. The one Stockard had sought out even boasted a picket fence—a luxury in a place where wood, for any purpose, was at a premium. He looked across the fence at the lights of the house through a scatter of brush and a spindly tree or two.

There seemed to be something going on this evening— every window showed yellow lamplight. Toward the rear, one particular window interested him. It was lit, like the rest, and a time or two he saw a shadow move across it. On an impulse, he stepped over the fence and went ghosting toward it to investigate, hoping not to meet anything in the shape of a guard dog. He reached the dark wall of the house without mishap and moved up beside the window, which was partially raised, for a careful look inside.

He had been right. The room appeared to be a sort of den or office, with heavy, polished furnishings that gleamed richly—a massive desk, tables and chairs, gilt-framed pictures on the walls. A man sat at the desk, half facing the window. He was dressed as though for a formal occasion; lamplight shone on the dazzling shirtfront and the flowing cravat with its pin like a drop of blood. Stockard put out a hand to rap on the glass but held it as the murmur of voices warned him the man was not alone. He lowered his hand and waited.

He could hear the voices but not what they were saying. One belonged to a woman, and by shifting his position slightly, Stockard caught a view of her seated opposite the man at the desk. And having once seen her face, he found he could not take his eyes from her.

She was a beauty—it was the only word for her. She might have been in her late twenties, certainly no older. The oval face, beneath dark-brown hair pulled back from a neat center part, held clear, delicately molded features and—most striking of all—large and luminous dark eyes. Whatever she and the man were discussing so intently, her demeanor was completely ladylike and composed, though her lovely face was animated by the urgency of what she had to say. Stockard thought she was making an appeal of some sort, and now the man nodded and, swinging around to his desk, brought a checkbook from a drawer and flipped it open. He took a pen from its holder, filled out a check, and used a blotter on it. He tore out the check and handed it to the woman as they both got to their feet.

Their words came more clearly to the watcher at the window. The woman said earnestly, "Thank you, Mr. Heywood."

And he replied, chuckling, "My pleasure, Nellie. You know I'm never able to refuse you anything!" Evidently, their business was concluded. The man ushered her from the room, leaving the door open on a hallway beyond.

Stockard faded deeper into the shadows and waited. Sure enough, a side door of the house soon opened, and an escaping fan of light gave him a look at the pair. He could see that the young woman was not as tall as her erect carriage seemed to make her—actually, not much over five feet, he thought. The man named Heywood seemed almost to tower above her. A few final words, then they shook hands, and she drew a shawl about her and turned down the path that led along the side of the house to the front gate. The man called out "Good night" and a moment later went back into the house, the door closing behind him.

Dan Stockard didn't hesitate. At the window again, he hooked his hands beneath the sash and lifted it wide; it was the work of a moment to slip through, avoiding the drapes that framed it. He had just lowered the window and was drawing the curtain when an exclamation from the doorway brought him around to find Heywood staring at him.

"Who the hell are you?"

"Stockard. I have a letter you sent me."

He offered it. The other man took the paper and glanced over it briefly. He had the rough and craggy look of a man who had worked hard rock. His hair was thick, iron gray; his nose lay slightly askew, as if it had been flattened in some brawl. The contrast between the man and the formal garb he awkwardly wore could hardly have been greater.

He asked a question or two and then, apparently satisfied with Stockard's credentials, handed the letter back, saying,

"You know you about scared the hell out of me!"

"Sorry. I thought it was agreed no one should see us together."

"Absolutely right." Bart Heywood looked behind him into the hallway, closed the door, and locked it. Afterward, he returned to the desk, motioning his guest to the chair the woman named Nellie had used a few minutes earlier. "So you're Stockard." From a drawer of the desk, he took a bottle and a pair of glasses. "How about a drink? I could use one after the start you gave me!"

"Just a small one, thanks."

Heywood poured sparingly and handed his unexpected caller one of the glasses. They shared a look over their drinks, trying to get each other's measure—one of them the operator of one of Tombstone's most prosperous mine workings, the other the man he had sent for and hired.

"I followed your instructions, and I found the house," Dan Stockard said, "but I was beginning to wonder if I'd get to see you tonight. The way the place is lit up—and the way you're dressed—I thought you might have something going on."

The other man shrugged. He ran a finger behind the tight, high collar and said roughly, "My wife's idea. She's asked some people in for the evening—Mayor Clum and the banker and a few of the other businessmen and their wives. They'll start showing up pretty soon, so this may not be the best time for us to do our talking."

"The young woman who just left," Dan Stockard commented. "She won't be coming to the party?"

"You got a look at her, did you?" The mine owner shot him a knowing glance. "Well, at that, I guess she's somebody any man would notice! That was Miss Nellie Cashman. Maybe you've heard of her?"

"I don't think so."

"A very remarkable young woman. She and her sister came over from Ireland, all alone, while Nellie was still in her teens. She headed west, and somehow she's managed to make it on her own ever since. She runs a boardinghouse and the best restaurant in Tombstone. But her main interest in life seems to be helping people who are down on their luck. Anyone that's sick or broke or both—he can always figure to go to Nell Cashman.

"Just now she was here taking up a collection for a fund she's starting for sick or injured miners and their families— like the man who fell down a shaft in the Lucky Cuss week before last and broke his back. And you can believe me— when Nellie asks for money for charity, nobody says *no*! The fact she's a damned handsome woman may have something to do with it. On the other hand, I've yet to hear of any man daring to get fresh with her. . . ." Bart Heywood paused, then abruptly changed the subject, setting aside his empty shot glass as he asked, "So tell me—when did you get into town, Stockard?"

"The afternoon stage. I'm signed in at the Cosmopolitan under the name of Dave Shaw."

The other man's head lifted sharply. "*Shaw?* Just within the hour, Johnny Behan was telling me about a holdup today that didn't come off because of somebody with that name. Would it have been *you*?" Getting a brief nod, he said, frowning, "Now I wonder if that was really smart? Going out of your way to make yourself conspicuous?"

"I didn't go out of my way," Stockard corrected him. "It just happened. Even so, maybe it wasn't too bad. It could save me some time if it helps word about me get around to the right places."

Bart Heywood looked troubled. He drummed callused fingers on the desk top while he considered. "Well, I'll have to believe you know what you're doing," he said finally. "I know of your record with the Pinkertons before you set up on your own. If I didn't have confidence in you, I'd never have offered you this job. So handle it your own way. Meanwhile, just what will you be wanting from me?''

"For now—information. Anything new since I last heard from you? Any evidence to change or confirm your opinion that Wyatt Earp is your man?''

"Well, you understand,'' Heywood said quickly, "as for hard evidence, there isn't an awful lot. There's been talk and suspicion. And there's the man himself. I understand you never met him?''

"No, I haven't.''

"Well, there's something about him raises my hackles. The man is one cold fish! What's more, I don't much like his reputation. He's full of big talk about when he was a lawman up in Kansas—at Dodge City and Wichita. But I've got my own sources of information, and what I hear don't always jibe.

"I'll have to admit that both he and his brother Morgan acquitted themselves well enough when they rode shotgun for a while out of the Wells Fargo office here at Tombstone. And I really haven't anything to complain about the way Virgil's handling the town marshal's job. But mostly that whole Earp clan is satisfied to be nothing more than gamblers and saloonkeepers; and Wyatt Earp dominates the rest. Frankly, they're nobody I want to associate with or introduce my wife to. You sure as hell won't find any of 'em invited to this party of hers!''

Somewhere at the front of the house a door banged, and there was a rumble of male voices and the lighter tones of women. Dan Stockard said, "Sounds like the guests are already arriving. Maybe I'd better go.''

"They can wait a minute. Anything else you want to talk about?''

"Well—for openers—what can you tell me about a holdup last March? The Benson stage. I understand the driver and a passenger were killed, but the shotgun messenger took over the reins and saved the treasure box."

Heywood wagged his head. "You heard about that, did you? You'll be hearing plenty more! Six months afterward, it's still the talk of the county—even more since the rumors about Wyatt Earp began to surface."

"Because of his friend Holliday getting in trouble over it?"

"That killer!" the mine owner said in a tone heavy with distaste. "Close as he stays glued to the Earps—to Wyatt, in particular—any trouble Holliday gets in is bound to rub off on them. One of the three men in that holdup was known to be an old-time friend of Doc's—a fellow named Bill Leonard. Doc had been hanging around with all of them, and on that day he rented a horse and rode out of Tombstone for parts unknown. Later, witnesses reported seeing him not far from where the holdup happened. Finally, along in July, a woman he'd been living with here in Tombstone—'Big-Nosed Kate,' they call her—signed a statement that she knew for a fact Holliday was a fourth man in the robbery and the one who actually killed Bud Philpot and Peter Roerig."

"So what happened?"

"Why, Sheriff Behan arrested him, but the case didn't hold up. First, the woman backed out on her statement—said she'd been drunk when Behan got her to sign it. And then Holliday testified that on the day in question he'd ridden over to Charleston, on the San Pedro, looking for a poker game. He even brought in a witness—Old Man Fuller, who has the job hauling water to Tombstone from the river. Fuller swore that they did meet and that Doc tied his horse behind the wagon and rode into town with him. That alibied Doc for the time of the holdup, and the judge had no choice but turn him loose.''

''Wouldn't that seem to settle the matter?''

''Maybe.'' Heywood shrugged. ''A man like Holliday—a man everybody's afraid of—stands to reason he could get a witness to testify to just about anything he wanted. And there's that Kate woman—she left town in a hell of a hurry. It was as though she knew, once she sobered up, it was no longer going to be safe for her here after she dared to tell on Doc. No, the talk ain't stopped at all, and more and more it includes Wyatt Earp—not only that he planned the job with Holliday but that he wouldn't be past using his connection with the Wells Fargo office to let out word when an especially good shipment of bullion was due to leave.

''I don't know if it's true or not, but I'm not the only mine owner that has his suspicions. I *am* the one who decided to do something about it—by sending for you!''

Stockard said, ''This Bill Leonard and the other two that held up the stage. I understand they've all since got themselves killed.''

''That's right. So *they'll* never be able to talk.''

''How were they spotted? Recognized by someone on the coach?''

''Oh, no. It was dusk; nobody got a real look at them. Besides—here, let me show you.'' Heywood opened a desk drawer and tossed something out onto the desk. Stockard picked it up and looked at it curiously. It was an odd sort of homemade mask, cut out of black cloth and crudely sewn in such a way as to fit over a man's head and across the lower part of his face. Unraveled rope had been added for a semblance of hair and whiskers. Worn beneath a hat brim, it would make a very strange looking but impenetrable disguise.

Heywood said, ''The posse found a number of these things on the ground where the horses had been held, and

Sheriff Behan gave me one. He suggested, and Wyatt Earp agreed, that the find be kept secret as a clue that might lead somewhere—though apparently it never did. But sure as hell, nobody wearing anything like this was going to be recognized, dusk or not!"

"Then what was the tip-off?"

"That was the posse's doing—the one real piece of luck they had. They managed to nab a gent who broke down and admitted holding the horses while the others were sticking up the stage. He was the one gave their names."

"But not Holliday's?"

"And the Earps right there listening?" Heywood grunted sourly. "Hell! He wouldn't have dared implicate Doc Holliday with all those hostile eyes staring at him! Whether he'd have stood up in court and done it is something I guess we'll never know. Seems Sheriff Behan turned him over to a couple of his deputies to bring in to jail and book—only, I guess they didn't keep a close enough eye on him. While they were going through their paperwork or something, the prisoner— King his name was—walked out of the jail, got on a horse someone had waiting for him, and left town. Nobody's seen him since."

Dan Stockard could only stare. "Do you mean to say they just let him walk out? What kind of an office does your sheriff run?"

Heywood shrugged. "You ain't the first to ask!"

Just then, someone came along the hallway. A heavy fist tried the knob and found it locked. A rough male voice demanded, "Bart, you in there? Man, we're waiting on you."

"Just finishing some business," Heywood called back. "I'll be right out."

The footsteps retreated. Stockard was reaching for the hat he'd placed on the floor beside his chair. "I'd better go."

"One more thing you should know about," the other said. "Wells Fargo's concerned as anyone about these losses, and I happen to know from Marsh Williams, the agent here, they've sent in an investigator—man named Fred Dodge. No doubt you'll be running into him. Trouble is, though he's supposed to be working under cover, about the first thing he did was make himself known to Williams and the Earps. In fact, he's got to be thick as thieves with Wyatt Earp, even dealing faro for him at the Oriental and using that as his cover. So if Wyatt is as crooked as I figure, he'll see to it Dodge never finds out. If I were you, I wouldn't look for any help from that quarter."

Stockard nodded as both men got to their feet. He pointed to the crude homemade mask lying on the desk. "Mind if I take that along? I just might be able to trace it."

"Go ahead," Heywood said, and Stockard shoved it into a pocket. "What else? Do you need operating money?"

"Not at the moment; I'll let you know." As the mine owner started for the door, Stockard interrupted him. "You'd better blow out the lamp, and I'll go out the way I came in. If I take this job, it's best no one ever finds out we know each other."

He was already at the window when Heywood found his voice and exclaimed, "*If* you take it? I thought that was settled!"

Stockard turned. "There could be one small problem," he admitted. "You asked if I'd ever met Wyatt Earp or his brothers. The answer to that is no. But once, five years ago in Texas, I did run into Doc Holliday."

The other man exclaimed in consternation, "You never told me that!"

"I'm not at all sure it matters. I was working on a routine case for the Pinkertons, one that had nothing at all to do with him. There's an outside chance, though, he might remember me. If he should—and if he has any inkling of what I'm doing here—things could get a little rough."

"*Rough?* With Doc Holliday maybe gunning for you? Good Lord, man! How could you even consider this assignment?"

It was a fair question, and Stockard answered soberly. "Because I need it. I need the money you're offering and the chance to set up as an independent investigator. If I can earn my pay here at Tombstone, I figure I'll be in business. As for the danger," he added bluntly, "any job I get offered is pretty apt to be a dangerous one. But once a man backs off from a challenge because of the risks, it can be the start of losing his nerve. I'm not ready for that yet!"

Heywood, still frowning, slowly nodded. "I guess I get your drift. If you're game to take the risk in facing Holliday, I can't do less than back you up." And he waved Stockard to the window and stepped to douse the light.

"One last thing," Stockard said suddenly. "That young woman—Miss Cashman. Where did you say she has her place of business?"

"I don't think I said," the other answered after a probing look. "It's the Russ House. Tough Nut and Fifth—northwest corner."

Stockard nodded, sweeping the curtain aside from the window. Bart Heywood blew out the lamp.

Chapter 4

Though full night had come, lamplight along Allen Street dimmed the desert stars overhead. Every saloon, and most businesses, were running full blast as though they knew no difference between night and day. Raucous sound poured out onto the street, where foot traffic kept up a racket on the sun-warped planks of the sidewalks. A rumble of dynamite blasting, somewhere deep in one of the mine tunnels that crowded the town and in some places actually undercut it, told that work continued around the clock down there. Even at this hour, a heavy ore wagon, loaded and outward bound for the mills on the San Pedro, rolled past Dan Stockard and raised a fog of powdery dust. Tombstone, it seemed, operated on a twenty-four-hour basis.

Moving through the district, he continued to sort all the information from his interview with the mine owner who had hired and brought him here. As he approached the Wells Fargo office, a man stepped out and pulled on his hat, and Stockard saw it was the local agent, Marshall Williams. The two men nodded, and Stockard paused to comment, "You work long hours."

"You're right about that." Williams sounded disgruntled. "I had to wait for the night man. That clerk of mine—

that Harry Phelps—he was in such a sour mood I couldn't do anything else but let him off early. I purely don't know what to make of that fellow," he went on, like someone with a grievance that demanded airing. "He's competent enough and has a grasp of the business. But at times he gets so moody, hell wouldn't have him, and I just have to send him home and tell him to come back when he's over it."

He changed the subject abruptly. "Well, you've seen Tombstone now. I guess you'll agree it's quite a town we've got." And as Stockard nodded, he asked, "You haven't changed your mind about the job I offered you?"

"Afraid not."

"Well, no hard feelings—that's your privilege. How about stepping across to the Oriental and having a drink with me?"

"I'd be agreeable to that."

But as they turned to step down into the ruts of the wide street, Williams caught sight of someone approaching, and he halted Stockard with a touch on the elbow, saying, "Wait up a second. Here's somebody I think you should meet." Stockard turned as a man came toward them with a woman on his arm. They met before the brightly lit entrance to a restaurant next to the Wells Fargo office.

Touching finger to hat brim, Marsh Williams said pleasantly, "Good evening, Sadie . . . Wyatt." And Dan Stockard looked at the man with sharpened interest. Wyatt Earp was bigger than he had expected—taller than Stockard, ramrod straight. His face was a trifle too narrow, his eyes close set, his jaw and mouth too hard beneath the tawny sweep of mustache. His slate-gray eyes took in Stockard with a penetrating stare.

The young woman, Sadie, came scarcely to his shoulder. She was dark, a striking brunette almost as beautiful—in a very different way—as the Irish woman, Nellie Cashman.

She seemed to take it for granted that a man would look at her. Probably not more than twenty, well dressed in a way that set off her womanly figure, she clung possessively to the arm of her companion and tilted her head in a bold appraisal of the stranger.

Williams made introductions. "This is Dave Shaw, Wyatt. He's new in town. Coming in this afternoon, he broke up a play against the stage from Benson and saved the mail sack for us."

"You don't say." The gray eyes rested on Stockard. They seemed to measure him and to note the lack of a waist belt and gun—Stockard wondered if the man guessed he chose to wear his weapon in a shoulder harness. Wyatt Earp had his own in plain view, an efficient-looking revolver in an oiled holster strapped against one long-boned leg. He said, "I been hearing something about what happened this afternoon. That took nerve. Maybe you ought to grab this fellow, Marsh. Wells Fargo could use a few such men."

"Don't think I haven't been trying," Williams replied. "I guess he has other things in mind."

"Oh?" Wyatt Earp's sharp stare continued its study of the stranger. "Anything in particular?"

Dan Stockard shrugged. "The best thing that turns up, I suppose. Isn't that what everybody who comes to Tombstone is after? Here I'd say a man's apt to turn up almost anything."

"Maybe. If he watches his step."

"I expect I'll be doing that, too."

The woman had stood silently by. But now Sadie, who had been eyeing Stockard coldly, appeared to grow impatient. She gave her escort's arm a tug and exclaimed petulantly, "Wyatt, do we have to stand here talking *all night*? I'm starved!"

Stockard thought she hardly looked emaciated. But Wyatt Earp's stern manner gave way completely as he answered her. He patted the hand that clutched his arm and said, "Then we'll just have to do something about that, won't we?" The scene broke up then as he gave Marshall Williams a parting nod and let his cool stare rest a moment longer on the stranger. "I might be seeing you around, Mister Shaw."

"You might," Stockard replied to this man, who was the principal reason for his being in Tombstone. And as Wyatt Earp and the woman turned toward the door of the restaurant, Stockard felt faintly uneasy, realizing how uncomfortable he had been during their brief exchange.

There was some quality in the man's uncompromising stare, something about the overbearing stiffness of his manner. In the past, Dan Stockard had occasionally met someone whose demeanor impressed him, only to realize later it was mostly a facade with little to back it up. And he wondered if Wyatt Earp was one of these hollow men—or someone as genuinely dangerous as he appeared. Perhaps time would tell. . . .

There was an exclamation from Marshall Williams. Stockard looked at him and then followed his startled glance. The door of the restaurant had opened just as Wyatt Earp's hand was reaching for the knob. Amid the clamor and the aroma of food that spilled through the doorway, someone stepped out, and they nearly collided. Then Wyatt Earp fell back a step, and the other man was revealed as Johnny Behan.

Light glinted across the badge pinned to Behan's coat as he and Earp stood unexpectedly confronted, both taken by surprise. And over Wyatt Earp's suddenly stiffened shoulder, Stockard saw the hatred that swiftly passed across the sheriff's face.

It was for an instant only. Then Johnny Behan's features smoothed out, and he smiled again with his usual dapper assurance. "Well! Evening, Wyatt. And Sadie . . ." He lifted his hat to the woman. "More beautiful every time I see you." She eyed him stonily as he made a half bow and drew the hat on again.

Wyatt Earp's voice held no expression. "You're looking well, Johnny," he said blandly enough. "World treating you all right?"

"I can't complain."

A lapse into silence then—no one speaking, no one moving. Stockard watched in puzzlement, aware of the tension in the Wells Fargo agent beside him. He sensed that the exchange of banalities was only a veneer overlying deep, unspoken feelings.

"Well—take care of yourself!" Still smiling, Behan drew aside and let Wyatt Earp and the woman go past him into the restaurant. Afterward, the sheriff gave a nod to Williams and Stockard and swung off along the boardwalk. He actually was whistling as he moved jauntily away and was swallowed up in the activity along the street.

As the Wells Fargo man let out his breath in a sigh, Stockard demanded, "What was that about?"

"It could have been trouble. Those two aren't exactly friends."

"They sounded civil enough."

"They had no choice. In a place as small and crowded as Tombstone," Marsh Williams told him, "at any moment, you can find yourself rubbing elbows with your deadliest enemy. You learn to speak soft—because a wrong word at the wrong time can start something you aren't ready for!"

"And what is it between those two?"

"The sheriff's job, mostly. Last year, when Cochise County was set up, Wyatt had been acting as deputy sheriff out of Tucson and had every reason to expect the governor would appoint him. But Johnny had friends, and he got named instead. The mines make this the richest county in

Arizona; a sheriff can collect something like thirty thousand a year just in fees alone.''

Dan Stockard hadn't thought of that. He whistled softly. "You could hardly blame Earp for being sore, then.''

"He's already served notice he'll be running against Behan in the election coming up next year. So you see, they were rivals even before the woman came into it.''

"I was going to ask you about her. Who is she?''

"Sadie Marcus. She's a dancer—I understand Johnny found her in a traveling show somewhere, brought her to Tombstone, and they lived together awhile. I'm not sure what happened—whether she decided he was never going to get around to marrying her or she met Wyatt Earp and liked him better. Anyway, she threw Johnny over and took up with Wyatt. She's an eyeful, but to me she's strictly bad medicine, especially with Wyatt having a wife already. But that's none of my affair. He and Johnny are both friends of mine, and I try not to take sides. . . .

"Well, what do you say we have that drink?''

Chapter 5

A drink was easy to come by on Allen Street, where every other building seemed to be a saloon—big, gaudy places or hole-in-the-wall dives shoved in between other places of business. The Oriental Saloon and Gambling Hall, at the corner of Fifth and Allen, was one of the largest and busiest. Entering, Williams started for the bar but then veered to look through the doorway of the gaming room, the source of a hubbub of rowdy voices. Stockard joined him there in time to hear him exclaim angrily under his breath, "Why, the sonofabitch!"

Searching the smoke-filled room, which was crowded with mostly occupied card tables, Stockard noted a table where players and onlookers faced the dealer across a faro layout. He instantly recognized one of the players—the man held a whiskey glass while fingering a slender stack of chips, frowning as he contemplated a bet. It was Harry Phelps, the clerk from the Wells Fargo office.

Marsh Williams said heavily, "I knew damn well, when I let him go early, this was where he'd end up! On the salary Wells Fargo pays him, he can't afford to throw his money away in a place like this!" He shrugged. "None of my business, I suppose he'd say. But it *will be* my business if he lets his work slide on account of it!"

"Nobody's fault but his own if you have to fire him."

"Yes, but I'd hate to do that to a man—especially one as good at his job as he's been so far. I've come to depend on Harry Phelps. Could be I depend on him more than I should."

Stockard watched the bets being placed, watched the dealer slide the cards from his box, watched chips won and lost. Harry Phelps scowled over his drink as his own bets were swept away. Stockard, for his part, was more interested just then in the man on the dealer's side of the table. He wondered if this would be Fred Dodge, the Wells Fargo detective who worked the faro tables at the Oriental as a cover. Marshall Williams, for one, could have told him, but the gossipy Williams was one man he didn't dare ask for fear word of his curiosity would eventually get back to Wyatt Earp.

They turned away from the gaming-room entrance and headed for the bar. It was solidly lined with customers, and a pair of aproned bartenders were busy. Finding a place, Williams signaled for whiskeys for them both. As these were being poured, he looked around and nodded to a tall man making his way through the crowd, saying pleasantly, "Evening, Morgan." Stockard turned to the man who nodded as he passed—a man whose resemblance to his brother, Wyatt Earp, could scarcely have been missed by anyone.

Dan Stockard watched the solid, broad-shouldered Morgan Earp work his way through the press. Taking up the shot glass of whiskey that had been poured for him, Stockard asked, "Just how many are there of these Earps?"

"A bunch!" the other man conceded. "At least four that I know of, and maybe more back in Missouri. Mostly, though, where Wyatt goes, the others eventually show up. Let's see now"—and he counted on his fingers—"the oldest is Jim—he got an arm crippled in the war. He's here in town—has a bar that he's operating. Virgil, of course, is marshal. Morgan took over awhile as shotgun messenger on the stages when Wyatt quit. Now he's working for Wyatt here at the Oriental as a house dealer.

"Come to mention it, I do believe there's still one more brother somewhere, name of Warren Earp. Give him time and I don't doubt he'll show up here in Tombstone with the rest. They're a moving-on family, those Earps. But California or Dodge City or Deadwood—wherever they do happen to land, you'll know they're in town!"

"Always ready for trouble?" Stockard suggested.

"If it comes looking for them. . . ." Williams tossed off the last of his drink and set the glass down. He wiped his hands on one of the bar towels and adjusted his wire-rimmed spectacles. "I'd better be getting along. Haven't had my supper yet."

"Another one before you go?"

"Not on an empty stomach. Thanks just the same," Marsh Williams said, and left.

Dan Stockard, who had no great love for whiskey and had already been given a drink in Bart Heywood's den, let his own glass stand unfinished. He listened to the talk around him while he reached into a pocket for his cigar case. Having selected a smoke, he bit the end and was digging for a match when he happened to glance into the mirror behind the bar and met the reflection of a pair of eyes staring directly into his own.

They were well remembered, for they were the coldest eyes—blue and unblinking—that he had ever encountered. For a frozen second, they met Stockard's in the irregular surface of the mirror. Then, deliberately, Stockard snapped his match alight and touched it to the cigar, turning his attention to what his hands were doing. After the first puff of blue smoke, he shook out the match and looked into the mirror—and the other face was gone.

Though it had been five years, there had been no mistaking, even in that brief glimpse, the gambler and killer named John Holliday, who, because he had been a dentist, was known everywhere on the sporting circuit as "Doc." But Stockard told himself there was no reason to believe Doc Holliday should have remembered him or taken any interest in a face reflected in the glass behind the bar. It could have been an accident, their stares chancing to meet as Holliday passed along the line of men who stood with elbows on the bar and their backs to him.

With casual deliberateness, Stockard pivoted and raised a bootheel to the brass footrail as his glance moved over the crowd. At first, he saw nothing of the man he was looking for. Then he caught a glimpse of Holliday passing through a door, which closed behind. He was still contemplating that door, trying to guess where it led, when he saw one of the aproned bartenders disappear through it carrying a tray with a couple of bottles and several whiskey glasses. On swift decision, Dan Stockard left his place at the bar and headed that way himself. No one tried to prevent him. He went through the door and found himself, as he rather expected, at the foot of a narrow flight of stairs. In an establishment like the Oriental, the drinking and the common run of gambling would take place in the public rooms on the ground floor; more serious activity would belong in private card rooms upstairs.

Stockard adjusted the hang of his coat, checked the gun in his shoulder holster, and mounted the stairs.

A reflectored wall lamp lit the corridor at the top. As he ascended, he heard the sound of voices, and when he stepped into the corridor, he saw the bartender at the doorway of a room passing his tray to someone inside. Before the door could be closed, Stockard shouldered past the bartender and moved through the opening.

The room was nearly filled by a round gaming table and by the men who sat about it. The poker game seemed only about to get under way, but already the air was blue with tobacco smoke despite the window raised partway, letting in the crisp night air of an early desert fall. Stockard looked at the men through the tendrils of acrid smoke twined about the shaded lamp hanging over the table.

Nat Gower, the stage driver, hailed Stockard, beckoning to him like an old friend. "Hello, again! Looking for a game? I told you Tombstone was a place you could run across some action."

Stockard hesitated. "All right if an outsider sits in?"

"Up to the boys," Gower assured him; but it was to Doc Holliday that those at the table all silently looked.

Holliday had broken the seal on a new pack of cards and was running them through his lean fingers, giving each a cursory inspection as though looking for imperfections or signs of tampering. His head lifted, and he gave the new-comer a slow regard—you would not have known from his manner that he had just observed Stockard in the bar mirror downstairs. Stockard met his look, having his first real appraisal of the changes a brief five years had made in this man.

He seemed gaunter, the flesh of his cheeks pared down, the hollows of his eyes deepened. His flowing mustache was still dark, but his hair was so generously peppered with gray that under the shine of the overhead lamp, it could almost have been taken for blond. Yet Stockard knew that, in fact, this man was still a year or two short of thirty—still a young man but ravaged by the consumption that had cost him a sometime dentist's career and turned him into a gambler and gunman and an alcoholic with a fatalist's reckless acceptance of early death.

Nat Gower was telling the room, "Gents, this here is Dave Shaw. Maybe you all heard about a little trouble we ran into bringing the stage in from Benson this afternoon. Well, this is the fellow that broke it up."

They all looked at the newcomer with keener interest. Doc Holliday considered this information and gave his verdict on a note of indifference. "We seem to have an empty chair. You may as well fill it."

As he drew back the chair and eased into it, Stockard was still trying to read Holliday's impassive features. He wished he had some assurance that the man really accepted him as a stranger, someone he had never laid eyes on before. For all he knew, Doc Holliday might have recognized him, and for reasons of his own, decided to let him believe otherwise. But Stockard had chosen a dangerous game, and he would play it out and see where it ran.

The man who had taken the tray from the bartender returned to his place, and now Nat Gower made introductions of the other players around the table. They were a mixed bag. There was a cocky little Sulphur Springs Valley rancher named Frank McLowery, who gave the impression of thinking very well of himself as a poker player and in any other capacity. There was another Frank—one Frank Stilwell— identified by Gower as a deputy sheriff in Behan's office. Beside him was a shifty-eyed fellow named Sid Whelan, with sandy hair and pale lashes and the look of an ordinary cowhand. Finally, the one who had bought the whiskey and was passing out glasses to the other players was an untidy, balding man named Wells Spicer, who, it seemed, was a lawyer and the local justice of the peace.

On the cut for deal, Spicer took the deck and shuffled clumsily.

As the cards started to flow around the table, Stockard took out his wallet and removed the slender sheaf of bills with which he had equipped himself. Frank McLowery said,

"That your table stakes? Maybe you ain't familiar with our brand of play in Tombstone."

Nat Gower spoke up quickly. "Don't let him scare you, Dave! The big stuff happens later in the evening. This here is just a friendly game—or what do you suppose somebody like me would be doing sitting in on it on *my* wages? A man can always feel free to drop out anytime the weather gets too rough."

Stockard had already decided that the big-money men Doc Holliday would normally take on must be busy somewhere else tonight—perhaps at Bart Heywood's party. Meanwhile, an inveterate gambler like Doc would make do with whatever action happened to be available. Past the drift of smoke from the cigar in his mouth, Dan Stockard said coolly, "I expect to stay in awhile." He peeled off a bill for the ante already on the table and only then picked up the cards that had been dealt him.

As play resumed, it appeared that Nat Gower was right— this was no high-stakes game. Dan Stockard, who was a conservative player by nature, had no great trouble holding his own. He won a few hands, dropped out of one or two he might have taken. Actually, he was less interested in the cards than in the men who held them and the talk that passed about under the smoke-streaked cone of light from the lamp overhead. As the only stranger, Stockard knew he was the target of unspoken curiosity. There should be some way he could turn this to his advantage, but when an hour had passed, he still hadn't found an opportunity.

The level of whiskey in both bottles had steadily fallen as the game progressed, with Doc Holliday seeming to put away twice as much as any of the other players. There was a break in the play then as men got up to move around and stretch their muscles. Holliday, holding up a bottle to the light and shaking it, said, "Here's a dead soldier. We need replacements!"

Stockard had very nearly broken even. Restoring his small stack of bills to his wallet, he said, "I'll leave word downstairs to send up some more."

The justice of the peace, Wells Spicer, had come over to stand near his chair. "Checking out, are you?"

Nodding, Stockard slid the wallet into his coat. "I've had a long day."

"And a busy one, I guess. It seems you're real hell on stage robbers!"

"It all depends. Generally, I try to mind my own business."

And now Nat Gower, his champion, spoke up. "Hell, you ought to have seen it! Dave, here, swatted one of them with the mail sack, and after that, he made a dive and got hold of a gun and sent all three of them packing!"

Activity in the room had suddenly ceased; everyone had stopped whatever he was doing to listen. "Nobody got any of the sugar?" Frank Stilwell asked.

That got the deputy a look from Stockard. "Sugar?" he repeated. "If you mean what I suppose you do, the answer is they took nothing except my watch. But it's got a silver case, and it's worth something, to me at least. And that's when I'm afraid I rather lost my temper."

"There were three of them, you said," Doc Holliday commented across the littered table. "And we're supposed to believe you drove them off all by yourself—single-handed? Ain't that just a little thick?"

There was a sudden stillness except for such sounds as came on the night wind through the open window or up the stairs and through the thin walls of the building. The window shade flapped once, unnoticed, with a crack like a gunshot. The players, all on their feet except for Stockard and Holliday, who still faced each other across the table, stood as though frozen in their tracks.

"Hey!" Nat Gower had found his voice, but it shook with alarm. "I was *there*, Doc. I know what happened. Maybe somebody in the coach did manage to break out a gun finally, but they was already on the run by then."

"Scared off by your friend the *big hero*," Holliday murmured, one corner of his mustache lifting in a hint of scorn. "Oh, they sound like a real bunch of amateurs."

Dan Stockard placed both palms upon the table and looked squarely at the other man. Holliday, for whatever reason, was purposely goading him, testing for a reaction. But without meaning to, he had also handed Stockard an opportunity that he couldn't afford to pass up, though the danger of it threatened to turn his breathing shallow in his chest. Deliberately, as his stare locked with the gunman's, he repeated the word Holliday had just used.

"Amateurs? Well, Doc, would you say they were any worse than someone who would knock a couple of dead men off a stagecoach—and then stand and let it roll away from him with eighty thousand in silver on board? What would a man have to be to pull a dumb trick like that? Blind drunk, perhaps?"

Someone in the room caught his breath—an audible sound. With every eye on him, Doc Holliday's head lifted. His cheeks, ravaged by the consumption that would kill him one day, bore two spots of color put there by the liquor he had been consuming—or perhaps by a sudden burst of anger that this stranger should have dared bring up, in his presence, the bungled holdup of the Benson stage.

But when he spoke, his voice held an icy control. "Obviously, you've been listening to some cheap talk, mister. I'll just say this to you or anyone else: Had I been in on that job, it wouldn't have ended like it did. No eighty thousand dollars would have got away from *me*! Drunk or sober, I'd have had sense enough to knock over one of the stage horses and made sure. And you had better believe it!''

And that was all. Though the cold blue eyes still blazed with anger, Dan Stockard understood that, for whatever reason, Doc Holliday had decided to let the challenge go. It was an uncharacteristic move—one that baffled every man who had witnessed it.

Chapter 6

Downstairs, Dan Stockard paused at the bar long enough to report another bottle wanted in the card room in the upper hall. After that, he walked out into the darkness of Allen Street, and as the saloon door closed behind him, the freshness of the desert night began to clean the smoke and whiskey fumes out of his head. Slowly, nerves and muscles lost their tension.

He had taken a risk, and he had got away with it. It had been a nervy thing to do, and repercussions were bound to follow. He could only hope they would work to his advantage.

As someone came through the door behind him, he turned to find it was Nat Gower. There was just enough light in the street to show that the stage driver's eyes were wild and staring.

"Game over?" Dan Stockard asked.

"It is for *me*!" Gower stepped closer and seized him by the arm. His voice was shaking as he exclaimed, "My God! What were you trying to do, needling Holliday like that?"

Stockard pulled free. "He started the needling. It got my goat."

"But—man! That was *Doc Holliday!* Nobody in his right mind even mentions that stage job to him—and there you had to go and throw it in his face! Couldn't you see his eyes? He was of a mind to *kill* you!''

''He didn't offer to.''

''But you sat there, cool as ice, and dared him!'' Nat Gower pawed at his straggling mustache while his head shook in disbelief. Stockard wondered what the man would think, to know how really far from cool he'd been when he took that calculated risk. But he said nothing, and Gower continued. ''You know, I got to feel responsible, me being the one that had to go and blab all that stuff about Holliday while we was riding today. I should've kept my mouth shut!''

''I would have heard it all sooner or later,'' Stockard assured him. ''One thing there's a lot of in this town is talk.''

''There'll be more now! Plenty of folks are going to be talking about what happened between you and Holliday, including those outlaws that hang out over at Charleston, I might add. They had them a pipeline to that table tonight.''

At that moment, a bunch of off-shift miners tramped by, their voices loud and their heavy work shoes rattling up a noisy thunder from the sidewalk plankings outside the Oriental. When he could be heard, Stockard demanded sharply, ''What did you mean just now? Are you saying that there was a known outlaw sitting in a game with a sheriff's deputy and the justice of the peace?''

The other man gave a snort. ''Mister, after you know more about this place, you won't have to ask such questions! In this town, a good poker game carries a helluva lot more weight than politics. A decent man like Judge Spicer can't always be particular who he sets down with. Even mortal enemies will put their differences on ice long enough to outstare each other over a fat pot of chips!

''You saw that sandy-haired fellow sitting next to me? That's Sid Whelan, and he belongs to that Charleston gang. He may be kind of small stuff compared to the leaders—

Curly Bill Brocius and his sidekick, a murdering skunk named John Ringo—but he's one of them, all right. And if *he* don't give them the news about you, there's Frank McLowery.''

''The rancher?''

''Him and his kid brother Tom have a spread where they run cattle and horses, not all of them their own. A lot of the ranchers in these parts built up their herds from stuff they got cheap after it was stole and run in from Mexico. Everyone knows that, but they don't talk about it much. Just like when you hear somebody called a *cowboy*, you're supposed to savvy it means he's really a rustler and God knows what else!

''And then that deputy sheriff—that Frank Stilwell! The rumor is he's held up so many stages here and there around the county, all the team horses know the sound of his voice and naturally *whoa* when they hear him sing out.'' Nat Gower stuck his tongue into a cheek as he considered what he had just said. ''Well, that could be a mite exaggerated,'' he admitted judiciously. ''But I'll tell you something that *did* happen.

''Couple of pistols held up the Bisbee stage just last month, and the passengers heard one of 'em tell the other to be sure and get all the *sugar*. Yeah, that's the very word,'' Gower remarked as he saw Stockard's quick reaction. ''So of course when they heard that, Wells Fargo never had a doubt who their man was. Virge and Wyatt Earp and a posse went out and picked up Stilwell, and by golly if his bootheels didn't fit the tracks one of the outlaws left. The trial's still pending, but Stilwell don't seem worried, the way he keeps right on using his favorite word!''

Dan Stockard had heard this in astonishment. ''And in spite of everything, he's still wearing his deputy's badge?''

''Well, you got to understand our brand of politics,'' Nat Gower explained. ''To hold his own in the election, Johnny Behan knows he has to depend on the votes from out in the county. That means the ranchers—and Stilwell is mighty popular with folks like the McLowerys and the Clanton boys and that crowd who ain't too particular who their friends are. So Behan ain't gonna let Stilwell go until he has to. Like when a court finally declares him guilty of stage robbing. Not a minute sooner!

"Like I said, Cochise County politics is something else again. The cowboys and their outlaw friends hate Tombstone because they were here first, and they figure the town has sprung up in the middle of their stompin' ground just to make trouble for them. And they hate Virgil Earp 'cause he's the town marshal, and now they hate Wyatt for daring to arrest Frank Stilwell—so there's a powerful lot of hate going around. But they're just *scared* of Doc Holliday. Wait'll they hear that a stranger come to town, got free with him, and walked away with a whole skin!" Nat Gower wagged his weather-beaten head. "Oh, don't worry—you're gonna be talked about!"

Which was precisely what Dan Stockard had wanted.

Moments later, the other man excused himself and went off along the street, leaving Stockard with a lot to think about—and, suddenly, feeling the aftereffects of that confrontation in the card room. The tension of it had taken more out of him than he realized, coming at the end of a long and tedious day. The next move could wait. Just now he had to admit that the bed in his hotel room seemed very tempting.

Stockard had taken a step in that direction when, all of a sudden, there was a disturbance inside the Oriental. He glanced around as, amid angry voices and a scuffling of feet, the door flung open and a man came hurtling out backwards, arms flailing. It was Harry Phelps, the clerk from the Wells Fargo office. He recovered his balance but was disheveled and unsteady from the obvious effects of too much whiskey. He swore thickly and made as though he would charge back into

the saloon, but a black-haired fellow with the build of a prize-
fighter blocked the doorway. The bouncer placed a hand
against the clerk's chest and gave him a shove, saying loudly,
"No you don't! You're out, and this time you'll stay out!
You been told the games in the Oriental are square. If you
don't like to lose, then learn to play better. Or try somewhere
else!"

Harry Phelps shouted something, his words incoherent
with anger. The other man cut him off. "I've had my eye on
you! You never come in here but what you end up drunk and
broke and raising a row. Now move along!"

Phelps sprang at him, fists swinging. The bouncer ducked
and, almost contemptuously, returned a heavy-handed clout
that knocked the smaller man off his feet and dumped him
prone on the sidewalk. He strode forward to stand threaten-
ingly over Phelps, saying, "You want more? You can have
it!"

This had all happened too quickly for Dan Stockard to
intervene. Now, as he stood unnoticed in the shadows, someone else came through the door. The voice of Wyatt Earp said
sharply, "Mike! Hold it!"

Mike said over a shoulder, "That guy from the Wells
Fargo office is making a nuisance of himself again."

"It's all right. Here—give me a hand." Earp stepped
forward and, with the bouncer's reluctant assistance, laid
hold of the downed man and lifted him to his feet. Stockard
caught a glimpse of blood—Mike's fist had opened a cut over
one eye. At an order from Wyatt, the bouncer shrugged and
strode back into the saloon.

It was curiosity now that held Stockard where he was.
He couldn't make out much of what Earp was saying to the
smaller man, who stood before him with head hanging, swaying
uncertainly on his feet. But he did hear him say, "I really
ought to resent you going on in public like that, about how

I'd allow one of my dealers to run a rigged faro bank. It ain't true, and you know it." Wyatt Earp laid a hand on the other's shoulder. "Your luck will change, Harry. But I think you've had enough to drink for one night. Go home and sleep it off. And get something done about that eye."

The quiet talk seemed to have done its work; all the fight had been knocked out of Harry Phelps. He mumbled something and then turned and started away. Wyatt Earp stood and watched him for a moment before going back inside the Oriental.

Dan Stockard left his place in the shadows and started to follow, staying a few yards behind the clerk and watching his progress. When, a few doors farther along, the young fellow moved to enter another drinking establishment, Stockard made up his mind. He lengthened his stride, caught up with the man, and seized his arm, saying, "I don't think you really want any more tonight, do you?"

Phelps turned on him with some of his former belligerence. "Who says I don't?" he challenged. He peered at Stockard and seemed to recognize him by the same faint window light that revealed the blood from his damaged eyelid. "Oh—it's *you*," he grunted. "The hero that saved the stage. . . . You got nothing to do with me!"

"I suppose not," Stockard conceded. "But somebody should keep an eye on you. You're not doing very well by yourself."

The other man was slighter than Stockard and, he judged, probably a year or two younger. He jerked free as he muttered angrily, "Get away from me! Damn you, I'm all right! I—" His voice broke off, his sweating face twisted in agony. Suddenly, he went stumbling over to the edge of the sidewalk and, clutching the upright of the wooden arcade, doubled over with a shuddering shout and brought up much of the whiskey he'd been drinking. Afterward, he leaned weakly against the post and groaned, "Oh, God! I feel rotten!"

"I'm not surprised!" Dan Stockard said. "You ought to be home. Where do you live?"

The young fellow muttered something nearly inaudible. Stockard had to make him repeat it: "The Russ House. I got a room. . . ."

"I think I can find it." Stockard took a firm hold on him. "If you can make your feet work, we'll get you there. . . ."

The Russ House was a sprawling adobe structure situated a block south of the town's center of activity. In contrast with the constant hullabaloo along Allen Street, things here were more or less quiet. The restaurant was dark, but the boardinghouse showed lighted windows. They encountered no one in the lobby. "Where's your room?" Stockard asked, and Harry Phelps mumbled enough to indicate the rear hallway. Stockard got him headed there.

Phelps was an awkward burden, his legs unsteady, his head bobbing on his chest. Suddenly, his knees lost all their stiffness, and as he started to go down, Stockard's grip failed. The man slipped out of his hands, fell against the wall, and from there to a sprawl on the carpet. He made a poor sight, his blood-streaked face turned up to the lamp in its wall bracket, his eyes closed. And as Stockard stood over him, preparing to haul the man to his feet again, there was a startled cry. He looked around.

Stockard hadn't been aware of Nellie Cashman behind him. The noise they made had brought her from somewhere, and now she stood looking at the unconscious figure on the carpet. Then she lifted her eyes to Stockard, and he saw them ablaze with anger.

"What are you up to?"

"It's all right, Miss Cashman," he assured her. "The man lives here. At least that's what he told me."

"Of course he lives here! *You're* the one I'm talking about! Anyone who'd do a thing like this—take advantage of a helpless person, trade on his misery and get him into such a state!" Her voice was icy with loathing as she stared him up and down. "You gamblers are all alike. I don't know how you can stand yourselves!"

Stockard straightened quickly, stung by this unexpected tirade. Even so, he could not be insensitive to the way in which the tinge of color in her cheeks and the fire in her brown eyes heightened her beauty. He wasn't pleased to have her take him for a professional gambler. "Miss Cashman!" he protested. "You don't even know me!"

"Sure, and I don't have to!" Emotion seemed to broaden an accent that was not ordinarily noticeable. She shoved a hand into her hair—an angry gesture. "Whatever *could* you be but part of that Allen Street crowd? A cardsharp, I suppose, or something worse. Oh, I know your kind—just waiting for another victim you can prey on!"

With that, she brushed past him and kneeled down beside Harry Phelps. She touched the swollen cheek beneath his injured eye. And as Dan Stockard tried to find words to answer her, she looked up and demanded, "Did you do that, too? Or just get him drunk, take his money, and leave the beating to someone else? . . . No, don't touch him!" she added as he started to put out a hand. "Sure, and I can do whatever is needed. I'll just thank you to please get out of my house!"

Dan Stockard pulled back his hand. Sharp words rushed to his tongue. Though he couldn't deny the picture she made as she knelt in the glow of the lamp on the wall, his feelings were momentarily overpowered by a rising indignation and an anger that matched her own.

Fighting for control, he said, "Miss Cashman, I've heard you're a fine person, and I don't question it's true. But I must say you seem a little pig-headed if you can jump to conclusions and believe the worst of someone when he's not done a thing to harm you! Had you bothered to ask, I could have told you what happened to this man.

"He was drinking and making a scene over a faro game at the Oriental, so the bouncer threw him in the street. That's when he got his eye hurt. I just happened to be outside. I saw the shape he was in and decided somebody should see he got home before anything worse happened. That's the whole truth," he added, "whether you accept it or not."

Her wordless stare gave no clue as to whether she did believe him. "Maybe," Stockard suggested, "when he sobers up, he'll tell you himself how it was—that is, if he's able to remember. It doesn't really matter."

Taking her at her word, he made no further offer to help with the fallen man. Instead, he lifted a hand to touch his hat brim. "Good evening." He turned and stiffly walked away past the faces that had appeared at a couple of the doors lining the hall.

The young woman made no attempt to call him back.

Chapter 7

Morning found Dan Stockard fighting a mood of depression, disturbed over that scene in the hallway of the Russ House. He blamed himself and his behavior. True, Nellie Cashman had jumped to conclusions, but he should never have let it turn into a quarrel. So he told himself, but he could see nothing to do about it now. As he shaved and dressed in his hotel room, with the busy morning sounds reaching him through the window that looked out on Allen Street, he considered plans for his first full day on the job. He would take things one step at a time, carefully feeling his way—there was no other program to follow.

Having finished breakfast in the Cosmopolitan's dining room, he went directly to Montgomery & Benson's O.K. Corral, one block west of the hotel, to rent a horse for the day. He had ridden better animals than the one they gave him—a dun gelding with a punishing gait and a mouth that had been toughened by many hard hands and cruel bits. Still, he knew the ways of livery horses, and this one suited him well enough. He inquired the road to Charleston and shortly was riding out of Tombstone and off Goose Flats, heading southwest toward the San Pedro.

It was a crisp October morning, dust devils walking

across the land, the sky busy with wind and scudding clouds. The air held a reminder that, even in this desert country, fall was here and winter not far behind. Stockard marveled once more at the clarity of the air, which brought the western mountains deceptively near—as though he were seeing them through a telescope.

Travel on the Charleston road was scant today, except for the heavy wagons hauling to the ore-reducing mills. Some distance out of Tombstone, Stockard noted an odd-looking vehicle standing beside the road ahead. Approaching, he saw that its strange appearance was due to a large wooden tank that had been bound with strap iron onto the wagon box. It was pointed in the same direction as himself but going nowhere—the raw-boned team stood motionless in the traces, heads hanging. It appeared horses and rig had been abandoned until, coming nearer, he discovered a man squatting beside it in the dust, doing something to a piece of harness. He reined in, saying, "Trouble, friend?"

The man glanced up irritably. He was an old fellow, with fierce brow and beard, and cheeks that looked as though they had been dug deep and cured out by sun and weather. His mouth would have been lost in the thicket of his white beard except for a rim of yellow tobacco stain marking its place. The cracked skin of his knobby hands resembled the broken length of leather he was fussing with. The old man was painstakingly punching holes with a clasp knife, and Stockard saw that he had some rusty baling wire with which to make a crude splice.

"Damned harness is too damned old and brittle," he said roughly. "In a climate like this, it breaks if you so much as look at it. Then I have to go and try to paste it together."

Stockard threw a leg across the saddle and stepped down. He could see that the ancient gear on the team horses fairly bristled, in places, from previous mending with wire. "I'd say you were about due to get yourself a new set."

"What with?" the oldster retorted, grunting over his labor. "Profit I make out of this rig, you could stick in your eye!"

"You're hauling water?"

"That's right. I took the contract for laying the dust on the main streets in Tombstone—they got wells for drinkin' water but not for anything else much. Job keeps me busy running back and forth to the river."

"I take it you must be Old Man Fuller—the one that alibied Doc Holliday and cleared him of a stage robbery and murder charge. . . ."

That brought the old-timer's head up sharply. Keen eyes blazed at Stockard. A gnarled hand slipped into the gap of his threadbare denim jacket. Next moment, Stockard was staring into a revolver that had been stuffed behind the waistband of the man's trousers. "Just give me one reason," he spat out fiercely, "why I shouldn't go ahead and blow your head off!"

"Someone you never laid eyes on before?" exclaimed Stockard. He had been caught flat-footed, and from the look of the old man, he knew he was in real danger. He spread his hands, careful to offer no suspicious move. "You'd better think twice before you make a mistake!"

Old Man Fuller gave a snort. His stare was implacable, his hand steady on the gun pointed at the stranger's chest. "It's somebody else's mistake," he retorted. "Ike Clanton or Curly Bill—which? Who was the bastard sent you after me? Hell, they knew I'd never let one of their own crowd within shootin' distance of me. So they figured they'd hire a stranger—right?"

"Not *me*," Dan Stockard insisted. "I never met either

of them. Never even saw this country before I came in on the stagecoach yesterday from Benson.''

"You were on the Benson stage?" The expression in the old eyes altered subtly. "Say . . . what would your name be?''

"Dave Shaw. . . ."

"Oh. *That* one!" Stockard saw the thought take shape. Slowly, the suspicion died. Finally, with a grimace, Old Man Fuller lowered the gun to his knee. "I heard about the holdup from Nat Gower—and what you done to bust it up. Don't seem likely you'd be the one they'd send." On the decision, he pulled aside his jacket and stuffed the gun back in its place. "Can't blame a man for being cautious."

Stockard drew a breath, more relieved than he would have liked to admit at having that revolver out of sight. The old man returned to his work. Standing there beside his horse, Stockard looked down at the bent shoulders and lowered head, at the crisscross of lines that age had scored so deeply across the back of his sunburned neck that they must surely be as painful as knife cuts.

He said, "You really think someone could want to kill you? Just because you gave Doc Holliday an alibi?''

"You don't know that crowd, mister! For one thing, I showed Ike Clanton up for a liar. He'd told some yarn about seeing Holliday riding hell-for-leather away from the holdup, and I showed there was no possible word of truth in it. But them cowboys must really have thought for once they had Doc Holliday where they wanted him. Ain't a one that's not scared witless of Doc, and with him out of the way, they'd have had a better chance to go after the Earps."

"And why are they so down on the Earp brothers?" Dan Stockard asked naively, curious to hear what the old man would say.

"Oh, you can hear all kinds of stories," Old Man Fuller

said, digging at the leather with his knife. "About Billy Clanton stealing a horse of Wyatt Earp's and starting a feud. And about Virge and Wyatt hauling Frank Stilwell in for stage robbery last month. But hell, they don't need no excuse. It's enough that Virgil Earp is wearing the town marshal's badge for the miners and the rest of the big shots that run Tombstone. It just figures that if you favor the old crowd and the county machine, then you *got* to be against the Earps!

"As for Ike Clanton, he's got his own brand of problems. Ike's pa was the head not only of the Clanton family but of that whole crowd of cowboys. When he got himself ambushed a couple months ago, Ike thought sure he was in line to take over bossing the gang himself. Instead, a tough gunman they call Curly Bill Brocius and his sidekick, Ringo, they moved in and just shoved Ike to one side—and he ain't even begun to get over it. He'd give anything for a way to change that, like getting credit with the gang for fixing Holliday or the Earps. I guess you'd say his pride is hurt. Though damned if I see what any Clanton ever had to be proud of!"

Stockard suggested carefully, "You don't sound as if you have much use for any of those people."

"No reason I should!" He stabbed again at the leather with the blunt point of his knife. "Mister, I got a boy, name of Wes. He may not be the brightest, but he ain't a bad sort, and I purely hate to see the time he spends hanging around Curly Bill and Ringo and the Clantons. I'd like to wean him away from them outlaws, but I so far ain't had any luck. Not a damn bit!"

And that would explain his bitterness, Stockard decided—his rancor toward everyone in the cowboy faction. In silence, he watched Old Man Fuller complete his work, pushing a length of wire through the holes he had punched, twisting it firmly. The old-timer tested the mended harness with a few snapping tugs and grunted in satisfaction. He got to his feet, pocketing the knife.

"About Doc Holliday," he said gruffly. "I told the court there wasn't no way Doc could have been in on that holdup because he rode my wagon with me that afternoon— tied his hoss behind and climbed up on the seat with me. Said he'd been to Charleston looking for a game but found it was all over before he got there. And he kept me company clean into Tombstone—too late to have taken part in any holdup."

"He rode with you often? A good friend of yours, maybe?"

"Friend? Hell! Before that day, he hadn't spoke a dozen words to me that I can remember. For a fact, it's had me wondering, ever since, just why he done it. This rig pulls slower'n molasses when the tank is full. Why poke along with me when he had a perfectly good hoss that would've got him to Tombstone in half the time? Damned if I know!"

"Perhaps you should have asked."

Fuller shook his head emphatically. "Pry into *Doc Holliday's* affairs? Oh, no, not me! Hell, no!"

"Afraid?" Stockard suggested mildly.

He saw the other stiffen. Slowly, Old Man Fuller's head turned until he was staring directly at his interrogator, and the fierce eyes were hot with anger. "Mister!" he snapped. "I'm no fool! Sure, I got a healthy respect for Doc Holliday—only an idiot wouldn't! He's meaner'n a snake. I been told I am, too, but that's different. *He's* not only mean, he's dangerous!"

The old man's eyes narrowed, his words underscored by the clenching of his fist.

"But if you're suggesting I'd stand up under oath and *lie* for him—well, you can go plumb to hell! Maybe you better, anyway. I'm fed up talkin' to you!" he ended gruffly.

Dan Stockard turned and lifted himself into the saddle. From there, he looked down at the old fellow standing by his

gaunt team, the mended harness in his hands. It was clear that
neither man nor the devil himself could easily sway Old Man
Fuller from his chosen course. "I never meant to get your
back up," Stockard said in way of apology. Receiving no
answer, he touched the rented horse with a heel and rode on
through the sun blast.

Like the other mill towns strung along the valley,
Charleston existed to process the silver ore hauled from Tombstone. The stone-crushing millworks sprawled over the barren
landscape, smoke and fumes from their chimneys fouling the
clear desert air. Just across the river, on the San Pedro's
farther bank, lay the town itself. It was a small place, a
scatter of adobes huddled beneath cottonwoods that made a
green oasis in the blistering summer season but now stood
bedraggled and half stripped of their dying leaves.

There were indications that someone had started work
constructing a wooden bridge across the river at the wagon-
road ford. But the water just now was low and muddy, and
Stockard sent the dun splashing across without even wetting
his stirrups. As he topped the opposite bank, he heard a
sudden swell of shouting. And as the unplanned sprawl of
boxlike houses came into view, he saw the gathered men and
the churning dust. When he heard a tattoo of pounding hooves,
he realized he had arrived in time to witness the climax of a
horse race.

Stockard pulled in unobtrusively to watch.

It was a match race, the two riders having set a course to
the end of the scattered street and back again. They had made
their turn and now were pounding back to the starting point to
the excited yells of their friends gathered there. There were a
good dozen of these, a loud and boisterous lot. Along the
street, more men and even a few women were watching in
doorways and under the arcades that shaded the town's adobe

buildings, but they kept apart from the noisy group at the finish line. It looked like the town's citizens preferred to let well enough alone and stay out of the way, letting the cowboys have things as they suited.

A wild-looking bunch of ruffians, he thought—most of them young, as most men were in this new country, their faces burned almost black, each with a gun in a belt holster. He wasn't at all surprised when he caught a glimpse of Sid Whelan among the rest.

The race wasn't even going to be close, and the rider of the losing horse seemed to be taking it badly. His friends called him Billy. He was big, though probably not yet twenty, his face thunderous with frustration as he whaled at his faltering roan with a short length of rope end, cursing as he tried to force a bit more speed. But he was eating dust at every stride, and he was getting a ribbing from the watchers.

So was a man who stood scowling in their midst while they crowed and laughed and pummeled his shoulder. Stockard heard someone shout, "Ike, I thought you told me your brother could ride!"

And another countered, "Hell, it's the roan! He ain't even good for glue. You Clantons might as well give him back to whoever you stole him from!"

The one who had to be Ike Clanton shrugged the hands away and muttered sourly, "You can all go to hell!" A stocky fellow, swarthy and bearded and not too clean, he was in a surly temper just now over seeing his brother Billy whipped by the other rider.

Dan Stockard reined away and dismounted, tying his rented horse to a roof support that fronted one of the town's saloons. Just then, the race came to a close in a confusion of plunging hooves and blowing horses and loud talk as bets were settled. Just before he turned into the saloon, Stockard again caught a glimpse, through streaking dust, of Sid Whelan.

This time the man was staring at him in recognition and surprise. Stockard gave him no more than a look and stepped inside.

The saloon was empty except for a bartender who lounged in the doorway with apron hitched up and hands shoved into hip pockets, watching the activity outside. Dan Stockard went past him to the bar, and with obvious reluctance, the man shoved away from the doorjamb and moved around behind the cheap wooden counter. Stockard ordered a drink he didn't really want; the bartender fetched up a bottle, poured it, and then waited, watching his customer finish lighting the cigar he had taken from the leather case in his pocket.

Three men entered the saloon.

One of them was Sid Whelan. He pointed a finger at Stockard, then stood aside while the remaining pair came on toward the bar. Stockard felt the hairs along the back of his neck rise a little as he saw the way they split, one moving up beside him while the other went a little past, to the upward side of the bar, where he half turned and placed the point of an elbow against the wood. Thus, they had Dan Stockard bracketed between them. He gave no hint that he noticed this or that he was at all concerned.

His cigar was burning to suit him. He shook out the match and dropped it and was reaching for a coin to pay for his whiskey when the man on his right told the bartender, "Don't take his money, George. It's on my tab. And pour me one while you're at it." The bartender spun a glass in front of him and filled it from the bottle. The man picked up his drink and pointed with it to the glass in front of Stockard, saying pleasantly, "Drink up, friend. This one's on Curly Bill."

Dan Stockard made no move to touch the drink as he looked at the self-appointed leader of the cowboys. Curly Bill Brocius didn't appear particularly dangerous at first glance. He was dark haired, fairly good looking, with a disarming grin when he wanted to use it. He was grinning now, but it didn't touch his eyes, and Stockard could sense the iron behind it.

He said bluntly, "I didn't know I was your friend."

The grin held. "Your name's Shaw, ain't it? You're the one twisted Doc Holliday's nose last night and got away with it? That's worth a drink anytime!"

"I suppose *he* told you?" Stockard indicated Sid Whelan, who was waiting by the door.

"He did."

"I've noticed some people make a lot out of nothing."

That brought Whelan forward in angry protest. "Hell! I know what I seen—what I heard!"

"It could be"—the one on the other side of Stockard spoke for the first time—"our friend didn't understand just whose nose he was twisting!"

Dan Stockard turned and looked at this one directly, gauging the mockery in him. He would have to be the man described as Curly Bill's right hand, John Ringo. There was nothing disarming or ingratiating about him. His sallow face and intelligent eyes had the look of someone completely unemotional, completely dangerous—as dangerous, perhaps, as the deadly Doc Holliday himself.

"Naturally, I'd heard of Holliday," Stockard corrected him. "But he made a remark I had to take exception to. There was no way I'd let it go."

Curly Bill smiled again. "Sid tells me every man in that room at the Oriental expected the roof to fly off, but nothing happened at all. You braced Doc Holliday, and he backed down!"

Stockard lifted a shoulder. "If that's how he saw it, why try to argue?"

Suddenly, more men were crowding into the room—almost the whole bunch that had watched the horse race, it seemed.

In the lead were Ike Clanton and his brother, Billy, the latter
a loutish, heavy-boned youngster who loomed a head or more
above his considerably older brother. When they saw a stranger
at the bar and saw how Brocius and Ringo had him bracketed, they immediately held up—all except Ike Clanton, who
strode to the end of the bar and dropped a hand on it,
demanding loudly, "What's going on?"

Nobody paid him the slightest attention. Stockard was
reminded of what he had heard: that Ike Clanton thought he
and not Brocius should have headed the gang after his sire,
the murderous Old Man Clanton, met his end at Skeleton
Canyon. Now, ignoring him, John Ringo told the stranger,
"There's something peculiar about you. From what I hear,"
he went on as Stockard merely looked at him, "you only hit
Tombstone yesterday afternoon, and today, here you are in
Charleston. You don't waste much time getting around."

"Anything wrong with that? Could be I have business."

"What kind of business?"

"My own." Stockard answered flatly. In the flyspecked
mirror behind the bar, he saw Brocius lift his head sharply.

It was he who said, in a tone that held a challenge,
"Anyone can tell you, friend, that Charleston is Curly Bill's
town. Any business at all that goes on here, I like to know
about it!"

Dan Stockard considered him, but all he said in answer
was "That's too bad."

Someone in the room coughed nervously, the only sound
in the stillness. He was keenly aware he was pressing hard,
risking real trouble, but Stockard was playing a role to a
definite end, and there was no point in half measures. He
kept any hint of inner qualm from showing on his face; his
hand was steady enough as he picked up his glass of whiskey
and tasted it. "Good stock," he said with a nod of approval,
and drained it off. Setting the glass down, he nodded again.

"Thanks for the drink," he told Brocius. "I'll be going along now."

Through every nerve end, he could feel the tension, and there was no missing the cold anger in the mirrored faces of Brocius and Ringo, one at either side. At the foot of the bar, Ike Clanton stood staring with his mouth fallen open, obviously waiting for something to happen. Now, as Stockard stepped away from the bar toward the blast of light beyond the street door, he glimpsed movement in the bar mirror. Without thought or hesitation, he came swiftly around, and the gun slid out from under his coat and into his hand.

He found Sid Whelan with a six-shooter halfway out of its holster. The man froze upon seeing a gun muzzle pointed squarely at him, and a sickly pallor began to spread across his slack features.

"What's on your mind?" Stockard demanded, his own face like iron. "Thinking maybe you'd get the man who faced down Doc Holliday? It's the second time this morning somebody's tried to pull a gun on me, and I'm getting tired of it!"

Whelan's lips moved, but no words came out. In exasperation, Stockard gestured with his gun barrel at the hand clamped over the holstered weapon. "Go on!" he ordered harshly. *"Pull it!"*

Given no choice, Sid Whelan brought the thing out, but cautiously, making it clear he no longer had any intention of using it. Stockard wasn't through with him. "Now toss it over the bar." Slowly, the man's cheeks became flushed, clear to the roots of his sandy hair, but though he wanted to protest, he didn't dare. With the eyes of the room on him, he laid his gun on the bar top and gave it a push that sent it skidding across the far side to land with a clatter on the duckboards behind.

"Turn around!"

As Whelan obeyed, Stockard moved up behind and took him by the collar of his coat. "I don't really like to do things this way," he explained, "but I'm sort of outnumbered. You and I will take a little walk over to the door together. As for my business in town, that may have to wait for another time. . . ."

He eyed the others in the room, wary lest someone else might be of a mind to challenge him. But no one moved, and now Curly Bill Brocius told him sharply, "Go on—get out if you're going. But if you're smart, you won't waste any time about it!"

Dan Stockard answered with a short nod. He kept Whelan with him as he went past the end of the counter, where Ike Clanton watched with an unreadable look on his swarthy features. The ones who stood near the door moved aside, out of his way. Just before releasing his prisoner, Stockard reminded Whelan, "Just remember, it was your idea to get rough!" He let go of him then with a shove and turned quickly to his horse. He freed the reins and lifted into the saddle. The gun was still in his hand as he sent the animal off at a walk, heading for the trail that led down the bank to the river crossing.

Dan Stockard had been lying. His "business" in Charleston, such as it was, had already been taken care of: He'd met the cowboys and their leaders and had given them reason to remember him. For now, he was content to leave them time to think about it.

Chapter 8

An invisible line in the dust split Tombstone's Allen Street. On the north side, which held the saloons and the gambling halls, a respectable woman seldom ventured—not even in daylight, certainly not alone. She left it for her sisters from the houses and the cribs to flaunt their finery along the boardwalks and hobnob with gamblers and idlers who frequented the dives and kept the town roaring.

South of the line, it was a different story. Here were the better restaurants and the stores and other respectable places of business. Here a decent housewife felt quite safe to do her trading, ignoring what might be happening on the other side of the wide dust strip with its constant and teeming traffic. And here, a week to the day after being ordered out of his house by Wyatt Earp, Nellie Cashman came shopping with Wyatt's wife and with his sister-in-law, Virgil's wife, Alvira.

She knew that what the men of the Earp clan took in was mostly spent on themselves; the women needed every cent they could earn with the sewing machine Alvira had brought with her from Prescott. Nellie made it a point to turn work their way whenever she was able. Just now she wanted new linen for her restaurant, and so she had asked them to help select the material from which they would run up a fresh supply of tablecloths and napkins.

The Earps liked their women to stay close to home—in Wyatt's case, Nellie thought, simply because he preferred not having it advertised around town he was married. The chance to go shopping was something of a treat for them both. In the dry goods store, they looked over the available material and helped Nellie with her decision. Then, while she selected other things she needed, they went off to look at some cheap ready-made dresses hanging on a rack at the rear of the store. They had no real idea of buying; they just enjoyed the rare pleasure of laying their hands on garments they hadn't made themselves.

Nellie was hardly aware of Johnny Behan until she saw the dapper figure of the sheriff standing beside her. Behan touched a finger to his hat brim, smiling. He nodded to the pile of purchases on the counter, but his admiring glance never strayed from her face as he said blandly, "Looks as though you're buying out the establishment."

"Not quite, I guess," she said, studiously polite. She had no particular liking for this man.

"That'll make a big load for you to carry, won't it?"

"It's all right."

"I'd be more than glad to give you a hand with it."

Patience was beginning to wear a trifle thin. "Sure, and that won't be at all necessary, Mister Behan. Thank you just the same."

He seemed not aware, or concerned, that she was losing a grip on her politeness. He leaned nearer, and now his smile bore a conspiratorial quirk. "But don't you think it's about time you and I got a little better acquainted, Miss Cashman? We live in the same town—we run into each other practically every day—and yet I still hardly know you well enough to speak to."

"We're speaking right now, aren't we?" She searched her reticule for the coins to pay for her purchase, using the opportunity to turn from her would-be suitor as she muttered, "I really see no reason to better acquaint—"

"If we were just to have a little time together," he implored, laying a restraining hand on her arm, "you'd soon see Johnny Behan is a real friendly kind of fellow."

Nellie had had enough. She turned the full force of her Irish scorn upon the sheriff, pulling away from his grasp as she grimly replied, "Very *friendly* indeed, Mister Behan! I'm afraid that's exactly the problem!"

Taken aback for once, the sheriff blinked and stammered for an answer. But he didn't get to make one, for at that moment, he was interrupted by a crow of laughter. And then Sadie Marcus was between them, and Johnny Behan's handsome face suddenly turned red with anger.

"Oh, that's rich!" the dark-haired girl exclaimed, her eyes blazing at Behan with scornful amusement. "That is damned good! Plain to see she wasn't born yesterday!" Ignoring the sheriff's furious expression, she turned and laid an approving hand on Nellie's arm. "Believe me, the less heed you pay to anything *this* man says, the better off for you! Especially if he starts making promises."

Struggling for self-control, Behan told her, "Nobody spoke to you!"

"He's great at promises," Sadie snickered, ignoring him. "But his real talent is at *breach* of promise!" she added, her tone turning bitter.

Beside himself, Johnny Behan half raised an arm. "You bitch! Will you shut your—" He stopped himself short, realizing Nellie was present. But all his dapper amiability was gone; his fist was knotted so tightly the arm shook. The beautiful Sadie Marcus faced him with a look of cool contempt, as though expecting and daring him to strike.

Half alarmed, Nellie Cashman put in crisply, "I think we've heard enough from *you*, Mister Behan!" That brought his arm down, the fist still clenched but the blow unstruck. He looked from Nellie to Sadie and back again, visibly controlling his anger as he sought the right words to say. But the plain hostility in both women told him he was defeated. Abruptly, he turned, heel leather squealing on the rough floor boards. He strode across the room, wrenched the street door open, and stormed outside, slamming the door behind him.

Sadie Marcus laughed, shortly and scornfully. "Congratulations!" she told the other woman. "You saw right through him! I only wish *I'd* been that smart once!" For an answer, she got no more than a look, without friendliness. She went on calmly. "You're Nellie Cashman. I've been hoping we'd have a chance to meet. I've heard a lot about you."

"I've been hearing about *you*," Nellie said without a trace of warmth.

"Oh?" The woman shrugged and tossed her head as though to show her indifference to anyone's opinion. "Yes, I'm sure you have! The tongue waggers of this town have been having a field day at my expense—all because that Johnny Behan got me to come here with a promise he never meant to keep. Like a fool, I let him string me along, until I finally got smart enough to see the light. And now *that's* over, they've got Wyatt Earp and me to gossip about!"

Nellie Cashman had let her glance move past Sadie. She said stonily, "I don't imagine you've ever met *Mrs*. Wyatt Earp. . . ."

Clearly taken by surprise, Sadie stiffened, then slowly turned. Mattie Earp had come up unnoticed as they were talking, with Alvira close at her heels. Face gone white, Mattie was looking at this woman whose affair with her husband was the common gossip of Tombstone. Talk of it had even reached the cheap little adobe house at the edge of the Mexican quarter where Wyatt kept Mattie, to tend his house, to wash and iron his clothes, to stay out of sight and out of his way.

Sadie Marcus returned the look, her own stare boldly curious. To Nellie, she said without a trace of remorse, ''I'm supposed to feel guilty or something? What happened isn't any of *my* fault! What would you expect me to do? Wyatt told me, right from the start, his marriage wasn't going anywhere.''

''That's a lie!'' feisty little Alvira spat out, loud enough to cause customers and clerks to turn and stare. ''Ain't a word of it true! You take it back, or . . . You hear me? *Take it back!''*

Without warning, Virgil Earp's wife flung herself at Sadie. Tiny as she was, she was full of fight. The Marcus woman backed up a step, an arm raised defensively as Alvira, sobbing with fury, tried for her hair. She caught a handful, and pins flew as Sadie was flung off balance, her handsome black tresses coming undone and tangling in Alvira's clawing fingers.

Mattie, stunned, could only stare aghast at her sister-in-law. But Nellie Cashman was quick to move. She caught Alvira by the shoulders and tried to pull her away, shouting in exasperation, ''Allie! Stop this! Let *go*!'' The smaller woman fought to escape, but Nellie's grasp was firm. Soon Sadie Marcus was able to tear loose of the fingers clutching her hair, though it cost her a cry of pain. In retaliation, she swung an open palm and struck Alvira's cheek with a slap that echoed through the room.

Allie would have gone right back at her, but this time Nellie Cashman managed to slip an arm around her middle and swing her off the floor. Holding firmly to the kicking, wriggling form, Nellie glared at Sadie Marcus. Her brogue had never been thicker as she exclaimed, "Sure, and if y'know when you be well off, you'll get out of here, or I just might decide to turn her loose!"

Sadie Marcus did not look particularly beautiful just then, her clothing in disarray, her hair down and streaming about her face. She was panting, her sweating cheeks splotched with angry color. She tried to speak, and nothing came out but an angry croak. Then, as she looked around and saw that they were the center of attention in a circle of curious stares, she realized the wisdom in Nellie's words. Angrily shaking her head and without another word, she made for the door as precipitately as Johnny Behan had moments earlier, not even pausing to close it behind her.

Virgil's wife was still trying to break free. Nellie Cashman feared that if she were released she would go scrambling after the Marcus woman to resume the fight. "That's *enough*, Allie!" she demanded. "Now stop it, do you hear?" She caught the looks of a dozen bystanders; from the disdainful expressions of the other women, it was all too clear that if this continued it would further damage the low standing the Earp wives already held in this town.

But the fight had suddenly drained out of Alvira. She ceased struggling and, when Nellie let her go, merely buried her face in her hands and stood sobbing. Alarmed, Mattie Earp placed a hand on her sister-in-law's shoulder and exclaimed, "Allie! Did she hurt you?"

"No, no!" Alvira shook her head vigorously. She began mopping at her cheeks with the palms of both hands. "That— that *tramp*!" she sniffed. "For what she said, I wish I could—"

"Please!" Nellie Cashman interrupted her. "Believe me, there's nothing you can do that would help." She looked past her to Wyatt Earp's wife. "I'm sorry! Believe me, Mattie, I'm sorry as can be!"

There seemed to be no fight, no fire at all in Mattie Earp. Her shoulders drooped. "It doesn't matter," she said, shaking her head despondently. "Nothing anybody could do would help." She drew a tremulous breath. "I'm goin' home. Allie, you coming, too?"

"Wait a minute," Nellie Cashman said quickly, "and I'll walk along with you."

The knot of curious onlookers began to disperse, seeing no promise of further excitement. Nellie turned to the clerk to arrange for her purchases to be picked up by someone from the Russ House. Suddenly, she heard a burst of gunshots somewhere in the town—three or four of them, spaced as though all from the same weapon. It wasn't too unusual for Tombstone, a place with so many shootings that it boasted of having its "man for breakfast." So she thought nothing more of it until, minutes later, she and her friends started for the door. All at once, running feet pounded the sidewalk plankings, all headed in the same direction. Then a man paused long enough just outside the open door to wave an arm at someone and yell, "Hurry up! This could be a big one! Looks like John Ringo and some of his boys are crowding up on the marshal!"

He was gone then, but Alvira Earp was left with both hands pressed to cheeks suddenly drained of color. Swaying a little, she gasped. "Oh, my God! *Virge!*"

She would have started forward, but Nellie caught her arm, crying, "No, no!" And then quickly to Mattie, "Don't let her go! Make her stay here. I'll find out what's happening." She waited for Mattie's nod of agreement, then hurried from the store. Somewhere farther along Allen Street, on the north side, she could see a crowd already beginning to form.

*   *   *

Dan Stockard—who had spent the past week gambling but not gaining much ground with his investigation—missed the start of the trouble, but he pieced it together later.

Apparently, a man named Jake Flagg—one of the Brocius-Clanton gang—had a jealous interest in a girl from one of the houses in the red-light district in the southeast corner of Tombstone. He had been in a saloon drinking and was in a sour mood, so when he saw the woman in question sitting with a rival and being too friendly for his liking, he evidently went berserk. All at once, his gun was in his hand, and he was out for blood.

The girl screamed and scrambled from the table when she saw him coming. The first shot plowed splinters from the table top. The room-trapped roar of the gun mingled with Flagg's curses and the yell of fear from his intended victim as the fellow's chair went over with him. Somehow the man got to his feet. Flagg, too drunk to aim, missed him cleanly with a second bullet. But he kept coming, and while the saloon broke into pandemonium, the other man turned and ran whimpering into the street.

Flagg came through the half doors right behind him; he punched off another shot, and this time he had some luck. Hit in the leg, the fugitive went down in a plowing tumble out in the middle of the thick dust strip that was Allen Street. There he lay, bellowing as much with terror as with the damage from the bullet.

Traffic halted. The swinging batwings of the saloon spilled out its customers, and from every direction a crowd gathered with amazing speed. But as Jake Flagg paused, teetering on the edge of the boardwalk, the crowd quickly split apart and scattered, leaving him there alone. They had seen the solid and threatening figure of Virgil Earp approaching across the wide street.

The town marshal's six-shooter was in his hand. He halted above the moaning shape of the wounded man and gave him a brief look to assess the damage to his bleeding leg. The tall man's head lifted then, and he sent a crisp warning to Flagg across the sudden stillness of the street. "One more shot out of that gun, mister, and I promise I'll kill you!"

Jake Flagg wasn't too drunk to hear the warning, but it was a question whether he was sober enough to heed it. And now, as he stood there facing Earp, his unshaven face a blurred mask with indecision in every line, a pair of men came shoving through the onlookers and moved up beside him. One was the sandy-haired outlaw, Sid Whelan. But the one who drew every eye was a man Tombstone held to be synonymous with danger—the gunman John Ringo.

It was he who said loudly, "Lay off him, Virge! The guy that got shot had it coming. Besides, you can see he's more bellow than bruised."

"Through no fault of his own!" Virgil Earp retorted. "Your friend was trying for the kill."

"No difference. I'm telling you to lay off!"

The angry words trembled in the dusty air between them as the marshal considered Ringo, a man reputed to be an educated reader of Shakespeare and the classics, a college man, and also a cousin of the murderous Younger brothers of Missouri. Just now, his hands hung empty at his sides, but that didn't seem to make him any the less dangerous.

Marshal Earp said, "I'm telling *you*, Ringo. You nor anyone else is going to say what the law in this town can or can't do. Do you really want to have a showdown—over *this*?"

John Ringo lifted a shoulder. "I'm ready."

"Hell, yes! Who's scared of *you*?" That was Jake Flagg, stirring himself to drunken defiance. "You Earps! You're all alike—nothing but blow! Now, are you gonna start something, or do we have to?"

That was the moment when Dan Stockard knew he had to make a move.

He had been approaching along the walk, almost at the entrance of the hole-in-the-wall saloon, when out of it erupted violence into the street. He had drawn discreetly out of the way, since it didn't concern him. Now, however, he saw something these men facing Virgil Earp were not even aware of, and on the instant he reached his decision.

A long stride carried him to Jake Flagg, and when the cowboy saw him and began a clumsy movement to bring up the weapon he was holding, Stockard's left hand dropped upon his wrist and forced it downward. At the same moment, the revolver slid from under Stockard's coat, and without hesitation he laid its barrel solidly alongside Flagg's skull. Cushioned by his hat, the blow was strong enough to stun and drop him first to his knees and then flat out on the boardwalk, the gun falling from his fingers and clattering off the edge of the walkway and into the dust.

Wary of John Ringo, Stockard turned quickly but found it was Sid Whelan who confronted him, his eyes behind their pale lashes blinking with shock and fury. "Damn you!"

Stockard cut him off sharply. "Before you do anything foolish, you'd best take a look!" He gave a jerk of the head, which drew Whelan's look past him. The outlaw's eyes widened as he sighted Doc Holliday coming at a quick prowl through the streaked shadows of building arcades that stretched across the sidewalk. "And yonder!" Stockard added, pointing with the barrel of his gun. This time, John Ringo also turned his head to pick up the nearly identical shapes of Wyatt and Morgan Earp closing in on them from that direction.

"You're boxed!" Stockard told Ringo harshly. "From three sides. Even you can't buck all the Earps, and Holliday, too! Yet your friend here would have blown the thing wide open if I hadn't shut him up!"

He saw horrified understanding flood the eyes of Sid Whelan, and even John Ringo seemed to be regarding him with a narrow and grudging respect. Meanwhile, the crowd appeared to know the crisis was over; the approaching gunmen had stopped in their tracks, as though sensing, too, that any showdown had been averted. And as tensions eased, Stockard let his gun slide back into its shoulder holster.

But as he did and as a murmur of talk began to grow and swell from the crowd that thronged the street, he happened to glance across the way. There, on the farther sidewalk, he saw someone he recognized: It was Nellie Cashman, and he was appalled to find her staring directly at him and at the man who was just beginning to stir from where he had been felled by a deliberate blow of Dan Stockard's gun barrel.

The note was slipped into Dan Stockard's hand later that day as he moved through the sweaty press of humanity in the main barroom of the Oriental. He jerked about, but he was too late. The evening crowd was dense; he glimpsed one of the aproned bartenders moving away but couldn't have sworn he was the one who passed the paper.

Jostled and elbowed in the noisy traffic between bar and gaming room, Stockard thumbed open the fold of paper and eyed the unsigned, penciled message. It said simply, *Come to Room 5 upstairs in half an hour. Come alone.*

He said half aloud, "Now just why the hell should I?" But even as he said it, he knew curiosity wouldn't let discretion keep him away.

Number 5, identified by the numeral painted in white on the panel of the door, was the same room where he had played poker on his first evening in Tombstone and had allowed himself the privilege of daring the wrath of Doc Holliday. Close upon the time appointed in the note, Stockard stood in the deserted upper hallway and narrowly eyed the closed door. No sound came from behind it. Tired of waiting, he drew his gun and, moving to the side of the door, gently tried the knob. It turned noiselessly; the door was unlocked. He gave it a nudge and let it swing wide.

He heard it strike the wall, so there was no one hiding behind it. And the oil lamp already burning above the round card table showed him in a single, careful glance that the place was empty. He entered, went directly to the table that filled the room's center, and after a moment of speculation, pulled out the chair that faced the open door and let himself into it. There was a deck of cards on the table. He laid his gun in easy reach, picked up the cards, and began to shuffle them, letting them run through his fingers while he watched the door and the hallway beyond.

Minutes passed. Then he heard the door slam at the bottom of the stairs, followed by the footsteps of a pair of men ascending them. Left hand holding the cards, Stockard rested his other on the table within inches of the six-gun's handle. He was sitting like that as the steps came along the hall. Then the shape of Wyatt Earp, with Doc Holliday just behind, moved into the doorway and paused there, regarding him silently.

After a moment, Earp nodded to Doc, who took a brief look into the hall, closed the door, and leaned against the wall beside it. Wyatt Earp came over to the table, and Stockard told him, "I got your note."

"You knew it was from me?"

"I took a guess."

Earp pulled out a chair across from him and eased into it. He indicated the gun lying on the table, saying, "You won't be needing that." But Stockard let it lie. He began working with the cards some more, idly dropping them from one hand to the other, shuffling them. Earp watched his hands for a moment in silence, and over by the door Doc Holliday eyed them both while Stockard waited.

"Quite a stunt you pulled this afternoon," Wyatt Earp said abruptly. "Do you always make a practice of interfering in things that are none of your business?"

Stockard lifted a shoulder. "I follow my impulse. It struck me those men didn't understand what they were being set up for. I figured two of them didn't matter, but I have an idea I may have spoiled a chance you Earps saw of settling for good with John Ringo."

The eyes in the narrow face hardened. Coldly, Wyatt Earp replied, "You got it dead wrong. My brother Virgil was doing his duty as marshal; that was all. But the rest of us stand behind him, and we didn't like the odds."

Stockard considered that and decided to let it go. He said, "I'm curious. What will happen to the one who was doing all the shooting?"

"Jake Flagg? Oh, he's sitting in jail for the night. Once he sobers up, he'll be turned loose and told to get out of town."

"And the man he shot?"

"The fellow wasn't bad hurt. The whole thing was nothing more than a nuisance, an argument over the favors of a whore. But I certainly wasn't going to stand by and see my brother killed for a matter as trivial as that."

That made a good deal of sense, and Dan Stockard

merely nodded without speaking. There was silence again, and he had an impression Wyatt Earp was measuring him. The muted sounds of the gambling hall came up the stairs from below.

The next question was completely unexpected, and it caught him off guard. "Would you be interested in hearing a deal?"

Dan Stockard's head came up as he studied the narrow face, trying to decide if the man was serious. "From you?" he exclaimed.

"I've had an eye on you these past few days since you showed up in Tombstone," Wyatt Earp said. "You turned down Marsh Williams's job offer, riding shotgun—said you had other plans. Yet all I've seen you doing has been to play a little poker around town—and from what I'm told, not winning a lot."

Dryly, with an edge of displeasure, Stockard commented, "You don't seem to miss much."

"I make it my business. I certainly didn't miss what followed after you busted up our play this afternoon. It was clear that Ringo and his friends didn't hold it against you at all for using your gun barrel on one of them—not when they understood it was done to stave off what could have been a helluva lot worse. You were suddenly the man of the hour. Even John Ringo was buying you drinks."

Stockard held up a forefinger. "One drink," he corrected. "I'm not much for liquor."

"Yes, I've noticed that, too. I've noticed about all I think I need to. . . . You ready to hear my proposition?"

"I'll listen, I suppose."

"As I see it, you've made yourself a hero, and now you should be able to write your own ticket with that cowboy element. I'd like to have you go to work on that. Arrange to spend time at Charleston and Galeyville and their other hangouts—after today, they'll be more than glad to have you. You like to gamble; well, you can generally find a game of some sort going at those places. Invite yourself in. Listen to what goes on."

Stockard was looking at him, the cards forgotten in his hands. "And—the deal?"

"Do I have to spell it out? You admit your luck hasn't been too good since you've been here. So I'll do this: I'll bankroll your game. Should your luck turn and you find yourself making a haul on the money I give you, that's all right—you're welcome to keep it. All I ask, while you're at it, is that you be my eyes and ears."

"In other words, you want me to spy."

"Call it what you like." Suddenly, Earp's gray eyes flashed, and his voice grew hard. "Damn it, that gang who used to follow Old Man Clanton is a thorn in the side of Tombstone! Now that Clanton's dead and they take their orders from Ringo and Curly Bill Brocius, they're the biggest threat to law and order in this corner of Arizona. And as long as I've set my stakes in this town, I intend to fight them with any means I can lay hand to!"

Earp paused, measuring Stockard's expression, then added, "Well, that's the proposition."

He waited, and Dan Stockard met his stare, framing an answer. Over by the door, Doc Holliday suddenly began to cough. It was a racking, rasping sound, painful to listen to. A handkerchief at his mouth, he leaned against the wall while lungs tortured by consumption fought to regain control.

As silence returned, Stockard looked again at Wyatt Earp. Slowly and deliberately, he said, "From what I've heard, sounds to me you're less concerned about law and order than in beating Johnny Behan out of his sheriff's job. In either case, if I came up with something to help you nip another stage holdup in the bud—and make Behan look like a fool— yes, you could figure that'd be worth paying me!''

He saw the chill that entered Wyatt Earp's stare, the anger that swelled his chest. And he found himself thinking, *Or is Bart Heywood right, after all? Are you the actual brains behind these bullion holdups—with Doc Holliday as your go-between and Brocius and his gang to do the dirty work? Are you maybe worried about a double cross? And what happens if I happen to learn more than you really want me to know?*

For a moment, he had an uncomfortable sensation that the man might actually have read his thoughts. But all that Earp said was "You still haven't answered. Do you want my deal or not?"

Stockard set aside the cards he had forgotten he was holding. "You put me in a ticklish spot. On the one hand, let's suppose I take your money and then can't produce any information worth passing along."

Earp ignored that. "And on the other hand?"

"What do you do if I simply say no?"

"Are you saying no? Is this a turndown?"

"The truth is," Stockard told him, "I just don't much feel like lining up with *any* side for the time being—if it's all right with *you*."

For a long moment, they studied each other. Abruptly, Wyatt Earp placed both hands on the table and pushed his chair back. Coming to his feet, he stood a moment longer, eyeing the other man, who remained calmly seated. "If that's your decision," he said crisply, "then understand one thing: Not a word that we've said in this room had better go beyond it. D'you get my drift?"

"You make it clear enough."

The interview was ended. Without further word, Wyatt

Earp turned and strode to the door, opened it, and walked out. Following him from the room, Doc Holliday paused for a final regard of the man at the table. Whatever expression his wasted features held was bafflingly indecipherable.

And then he, too, was gone. Though Dan Stockard was alone again, Wyatt Earp's final warning seemed to hang in the room like something almost tangible.

Chapter 9

In morning sunlight that still held the chill of the previous night, Dan Stockard stood indecisively before the entrance of the Russ House. The impulse that brought him here had been strong enough, but now he was less certain. He frowned as he breathed in the scent of piñon pine smoke from morning cook fires, which lingered in layers on the autumn air above Tombstone. He said aloud, "If you don't do it now, you never will. You'll always know you lacked the nerve for something that absolutely needed to be done." Thus scolded by his own conscience, he opened the door and stepped inside the building, pulling off his hat as he entered.

The lobby was deserted except for a woman, with skirts pinned up and sleeves rolled to her elbows, who was using a rag to rid the furniture of the dust that constantly settled over everything in this town. She wasn't Nellie Cashman, however. When she straightened and turned to look at him, he saw this was another woman, worn and sad-faced, with the dark stains of grief beneath her eyes making her appear older than she probably was.

"Yes?" she said. "Did you want something?"

"To see Miss Cashman, if it's possible."

The woman frowned uncertainly, turning the dust rag in

her hands. "I just don't know. I'm afraid Nellie didn't get a chance for much sleep last night. She was taking care of one of her boarders that's come down with pneumonia."

"I see. . . ."

"If it's about a room—"

"No," Stockard said quickly. "Not a room. A personal matter. But—well, after what you tell me, it doesn't seem all that important. Not important enough to bother her with."

"Would you want to leave a message?" the woman asked.

"I guess not," he said, and he turned again for the door. "No message."

His hand was on the latch when a voice he vividly remembered spoke from the inner hallway. "You were looking for me?"

He turned back, hat still in hand. Nellie Cashman stood in the hall doorway with a stack of linen folded over one arm. For someone who had had a sleepless night, she appeared as neat and as freshly groomed as he had ever seen her. Dan Stockard hesitated. "Yes, I was. But—"

"We can talk here," she suggested. If he had expected to find her icy and contemptuous, as on the previous occasion, he was surprised; her manner was polite and seemingly without rancor.

The woman who had been cleaning the room asked, "Shall I take those things, Nellie?"

"If you will, Hazel. Thank you." She handed over the armload of linen, and the other woman disappeared into the back part of the building. Nellie Cashman stepped forward into the lobby.

For a moment, she and Stockard looked at each other, neither speaking. Finally, he said, "I'm afraid I picked a bad time. I understand there's someone down with pneumonia."

"He's going to be all right," she assured him quickly.

"Dr. Goodfellow was here just now, and he says the fever's broken. The worst is over."

"Glad to hear it," Stockard said, and another silence began. It seemed to bother them both. Suddenly, both began to speak at the same time and broke off again as their words collided.

Taking a breath, Dan Stockard ended the deadlock. "Miss Cashman," he said, "I'm here because I couldn't go any longer without trying to apologize for the other night. I'm afraid I lost my temper because you jumped to a conclusion that was perfectly natural under the circumstances. At any rate, I should never have talked to you the way I did. I'm sorry."

"No—please!" She lifted a hand. The brown eyes seemed enormous and filled with real concern. To his astonishment, she continued, in her delightful Irish brogue, "Believe me, *I'm* the one who should be apologizing, Mister Shaw—yes, as you can see, I've learned your name. That night, even as you were walking away, I knew I must have made a mistake. So next day, when he was himself again, I did as you told me. I talked to Harry Phelps, and he gave me the truth about you.

"He assured me you had nothing at all to do with his getting himself into trouble that evening, that you only stepped in to try and see him home in one piece. And I've been hoping ever since to see you again, to tell you how ashamed it is I am for tearing into you without knowing what I was talking about or giving you a chance to explain."

"But what about yesterday?" Stockard exclaimed. "What you must have thought when you saw me use a gun barrel to club a man senseless!"

"Why, it was clear to me there'd likely been a massacre if you hadn't—what with the way those Earps were moving in. You had to move fast if you were to save your friends. Isn't that right?''

"Something like that. Only those weren't friends, Miss Cashman. The one I hit was nobody I'd ever laid eyes on, so far as I know—just a petty outlaw that hangs out with the Clantons and Curly Bill Brocius. You haven't much of an opinion of me if you think that's the kind I belong with!''

"Is my opinion that important?''

"I'm beginning to realize few things are more important—at least to me!'' he heard himself declare bluntly, and when he saw her reaction—the way she stared at him—he was suddenly embarrassed by his brashness. He took a step toward the door as he added, "I guess I've said what I came for—and a good deal more than I should have. I thank you for hearing me out. I won't bother you any longer.''

But again she stopped him. "Please! You aren't *bothering* me, as you put it. There's something more I'd like to talk to you about. That is, if you can spare a few minutes.''

"Of course.''

"Why don't we sit down?''

There was an ancient but comfortable-looking sofa near the window, and she invited him to join her. He placed his hat on the floor beside his boot as he sat down. It was pleasantly quiet here; though Tombstone never stopped or even slowed down, Sunday or any other day, the busy boomtown racket reached this quiet lobby as nothing more than a distant murmur of sound.

Nellie Cashman folded her hands in her lap. "You understand, I don't like to interfere in a thing that is none of my business, though I'm afraid I have a reputation for doing just that! It's my nature, I guess, when I see someone in trouble and there might be some way I can help. At any rate, I wanted to ask you about poor Harry Phelps.''

Stockard thought he understood. "You mean, about what

really happened the other night?'' he asked, and she nodded. ''There's nothing much you don't already know. He dropped some money at the faro table in the Oriental and afterward claimed he'd been cheated, and he raised such a fuss they had to throw him out. He got his face cut up some in the process. That's when I stepped in.''

Nellie sighed. ''I really worry about him. Harry came out here from someplace in the East thinking Tombstone would be a place of opportunity for a young man with ambition. It just hasn't worked out the way he hoped. I think he works very hard at his job, but he feels he isn't getting anywhere in that Wells Fargo office.''

''I can understand that. His boss told me the fellow's almost indispensable, yet the company won't pay him what he's worth. On the other hand, Williams isn't all that pleased to see the way he spends his spare time.''

''But Harry gets discouraged,'' Nellie explained. ''And when he does, he kicks over the traces and drinks too much and gambles more than he can afford to lose. Seeing it just makes me feel terrible!''

''Well, he's a grown man, Miss Cashman. Nobody can be his nursemaid—he's got to stand or fall on his own. This is a hard country,'' Stockard pointed out. ''It doesn't make allowances. . . . But I don't have to tell *you* that. Not someone who's taken care of herself the way you have, completely alone, and somehow managed to carry other people's burdens while you were at it. It's no wonder the people of Tombstone call you 'the miners' angel.' ''

She frowned and made an impatient gesture with one hand. ''That's just malarkey!'' she exclaimed in her broadest brogue. ''Sure, and I've only tried to be an honest Christian. And I've been luckier than I deserved!''

''I sort of doubt that.''

''Oh, but it's true! All I have to do is look around and

see the awful things that happen to other people. Like that poor Hazel Roerig you met just now. Six months ago, her husband was killed, and the poor woman is lost without him—and her with two little children to boot. I'm so sorry for them all! Naturally, I'm seeing that they have a place to stay as long as they need it and until Hazel can get on top of things. Still, you saw the way she insists on trying to pay me back, helping out in whatever little way she can even though I've told her I wish she wouldn't. . . ."

"Roerig?" Stockard repeated. "Is she the widow of the man who was killed on the Benson stage during a holdup last March?"

Nellie's generous mouth tightened. "Yes! Shot by that murdering Doc Holliday!"

"You sound very sure of that."

"That he's a murderer? It's general knowledge, isn't it?" she insisted grimly. "His reputation follows him. And he's killed at least one man right here in Tombstone!"

"I meant about the holdup. You seem convinced he was in on it, that he was the one who shot Pete Roerig and probably the driver, too, even though he was cleared of the charge."

"Sure, and the law can make mistakes, can't it?" Nellie rejoined in fine spirit. The next moment, however, her brown eyes were frowning at him thoughtfully as she said, "Mister Shaw, I can't help wondering why you should be interested in this. *I* am, naturally, because of my friend Hazel. But you're a stranger. And that all happened—why, months ago. I really don't understand."

Stockard hesitated. It was one thing to put on a front with Wyatt Earp and Doc Holliday and with the outlaws who followed Curly Bill Brocius. But deliberately deceiving a person like Nellie Cashman was a different matter. He drew a breath.

"Before I try to answer that," he said, his course suddenly chosen, "let me first ask *you* a question. Exactly what is your impression of me? Do I seem to you an adventurer of some kind—a professional gambler, perhaps?" And when she seemed reluctant to answer, he added quickly, "Because that's just what I've been wanting people here to think. But not you! You likely haven't given the thing much thought, but to me it matters very much that you should have a better opinion of me than that! Besides, I know you can be trusted to keep to yourself anything I might tell you."

"Well, of course!" she exclaimed. The color had heightened in her cheeks; suddenly, she was almost stammering. "But my goodness! I didn't realize I was *prying*! I ought not to have asked you that, Mister Shaw!"

"I'm glad you did! Because I haven't told you the truth." His decision made, he plunged ahead. "First of all, my name's not Shaw. It's Stockard. Dan Stockard. And I'm a detective."

"A Pinkerton man?" she asked, her eyes widening.

"No. I'm what's known as a private investigator. I used to work for the Pinkertons, but I didn't care for some of their methods. I thought I could do a better job on my own. And actually that's what I'm testing now—I'm here working on my first assignment."

"You're investigating that holdup!" she exclaimed with quick understanding.

"Among others. The party who hired me has a real stake in the situation. I can't give you his name, but this person is convinced he knows who has been responsible for masterminding at least some of the raids on the treasure coaches out of Tombstone. So far, he has nothing but rumors and suspicions. I'm supposed to find the proof that will either convict that man or clear him."

"I think," Nellie said flatly, "you mean Wyatt Earp." And there was no warmth in her voice.

"You've heard the rumors, then. You sound as if you believe them."

"I wish I didn't!" The hands in her lap tightened into fists. "I think of those poor women!" she explained with a rush, seeing his questioning look. "Wyatt's wife, Mattie. And, yes, even Virgil's Allie, though I do think Virge loves her. He's not the kind who would humiliate his wife like Wyatt does, showing off that Sadie Marcus woman in front of the whole town!

"But at best it hasn't been easy for anyone married into that Earp family! Ordered around by their men, looked down on by all those women who think themselves better than anyone else. . . . If it should turn out that the head of the clan is actually a thief—" She shook her head in dismay over the thought.

Stockard frowned. "Are you telling me you wish I wouldn't do my job?"

"Oh, no—of course not!" In her earnestness, she placed a hand on his and let it rest there. "Obviously, someone has to stop what's going on, whoever might turn out to be involved! And so far neither Wells Fargo nor the sheriff's office have managed at all. At the same time," she added seriously, "I'm sure you must realize the danger you'll be in if the wrong people find out who you are and what you're up to!"

"I'm not too worried. Like you, I've generally been able to look out for myself. I take precautions. . . ." And he pulled his coat back to show her the gun in its spring holster, strapped beneath his arm.

He wasn't prepared for her reaction. She looked at the gun, and she made a smothered exclamation. *"Oh. . . ."* A look of revulsion clouded her lovely face; she snatched back her hand from Stockard's.

Somehow it hadn't occurred to him that someone so long familiar with the frontier and accustomed to its violence would have such an aversion to firearms. Or had it been the manner in which he'd cold-bloodedly sprung the subject on her? He silently cursed his clumsiness as he picked up his hat and got hastily to his feet.

Stockard took a few paces across the lobby, pulling on his hat. Then he turned back to say, stiffly, "I thank you for your time. It's been frustrating—almost no results since I've been here. I keep working and prying, but so far no luck at all."

Whatever emotion had troubled her, she seemed to have overcome it. Unexpectedly, she asked him, "Is there any way I could help?"

"No!" he said almost fiercely. "If there was, I couldn't ask it! It's too dangerous a game I'm in. The last thing I'd want is any risk of you getting involved."

"Why, as for that," Nellie said with a bare hint of a smile, "I've already been accused of spying." On seeing his questioning look, she explained. "Wyatt Earp did it and ordered me out of his house. It was when I brought Allie a letter, sent in care of the Russ House, from Kate Holliday."

For an instant, the name failed to register. Then Stockard exclaimed, "You wouldn't mean—Doc Holliday's Kate? The one who disappeared after she signed that paper charging him with the Benson holdup? Are you saying you know what became of her?"

"Why, yes, I know where she is. It's a secret, though, not only from Doc but from Wyatt, too. I'm convinced she left Tombstone in a hurry because she was afraid to stay."

"But she could hold the key to this whole situation!"

Then he added, doubtfully, "Though I don't suppose she'll be apt to do any talking to a total stranger!"

Nellie saw the direction of his thinking. "She'd trust *me,* I think, if I were with you and we caught her in the right mood. . . ."

Dan Stockard stared at her. "You'd do this?"

"Why not?" She rose and moved to face him. "It's worth a try. Depending on how she feels now about Doc Kate couldn't do any more than refuse." She hesitated. "But of course you'd have to promise you won't betray her secret."

"Naturally!"

"Very well, then. Kate is in Globe, running a boarding-house there. If you want to try talking to her, there's no reason I couldn't get away for a few days, now that my pneumonia patient is out of danger. I'll call it a business trip. In fact, there are people in Tucson I've been wanting to see for contributions to a miners' fund I'm starting, and that would be on the way. I can be ready to leave this afternoon."

"Thank you!" In his gratitude, he seized both her hands. They were strong and warm, the capable hands of a woman who had made her own way and fought her own battles, yet had given gentle and tender care to those who needed it. For a moment, they stood like that, and Nellie made no move to withdraw. It was Stockard who released her, saying gruffly, "Till this afternoon, then. I'll see you at the stage. It's best if we don't seem to be together."

"Of course," she agreed promptly.

Chapter 10

That afternoon, at the Wells Fargo depot, Nellie appeared in a simple but becoming traveling dress and bonnet, carrying a small bag. Stockard tipped his hat but otherwise gave her no more attention than any of the half-dozen other passengers waiting to board the coach for Benson. Once again, the driver would be the yellow-haired Nat Gower. He greeted Stockard warmly but then said, "Leaving town, are you? Things getting a little too warm for you here in Tombstone?"

"I expect to be back in a few days," Stockard assured him. "Business proposition I have to look into; with my luck, it probably won't come to anything." He added, "If you're not carrying a shotgun messenger, I'd like to ride up top. Or do you think I might get us held up again?"

"If that don't bother you, *I* ain't worried. Go ahead— climb aboard. . . ."

Apparently, no one took Dan Stockard for a shotgun messenger, and the run to Benson was made without incident. An early-autumn dusk had descended, and its chill lay upon the land. There was time for a restaurant meal, Stockard and Nellie Cashman still keeping up the pretense of being strangers. When the westbound train for Tucson pulled in, filling the station with the glare of its headlamp, the noise of its bell, and with escaping steam as drive wheels punished the tracks, they mounted the single day coach along with the other waiting passengers and found separate seats.

It was almost eight o'clock when they pulled into the station at Tucson, where they learned the twice-a-week stage run to Globe would leave at first light. They checked into separate rooms at a hotel near the railroad yards, and Nellie went about her task of collecting charitable funds from the people she had come to see. When she and Stockard met again, at breakfast, she was able to announce some good results.

At the stage station, they found that none of yesterday's fellow passengers would be sharing this final leg of the journey. Accordingly, they no longer needed to pretend at being strangers but took a seat together. They left Tucson on the road north to Globe under a cloud sheet that had slid across the sky during the night. A boisterous wind raked the landscape and buffeted the coach, making the leather window curtains pop against their moorings like rifle shots.

There were two other travelers to share the coach with them. They were a youthful couple, just married. The man was a mining engineer on his way to Globe to take a job that, Stockard gathered, had been arranged for him through wealthy connections. His bride was a Boston girl, very young and obviously away from home for the first time. She clung to her husband's arm and listened admiringly to his talk, but Stockard sensed the timidity with which she looked through the window upon a tortured and forbidding landscape, so very different from anything she had ever known.

Almost the only time she spoke was to ask Nellie, with polite interest, "And you and your husband? Do you live in Globe?"

Nellie smiled a little at the mistake. "No. Actually, we aren't together. We're not married—just acquaintances."

"Oh!" The girl turned rosy with embarrassment. "I'm sorry! Since *we* are, I—I guess I just supposed that everybody—" She broke off in confusion.

Nellie smiled again and shook her head. "No need to apologize. I understand."

Later, when they pulled into a station for the driver to pick up fresh teams and check the running gear of the coach, Stockard had a few moments alone with Nellie. As they stood together in the windswept open near the adobe building, he said, "I hope it didn't bother you, having us taken for man and wife."

Not looking at him, she said briefly, "It's all right."

"I guess it was more or less a natural mistake—a flattering one, for me!" he added impulsively. "But anyone seeing an attractive young woman in this country would naturally take it for granted she was spoken for."

That raised Nellie's head; she gave him a long and level look. "Are you asking why I'm *not* married?"

"I'm not asking anything," Stockard quickly assured her. "Though I have to admit, I'm intrigued by almost everything I do know about you."

"I suppose," she said slowly, apparently deciding to answer her own question, "not all marriages have to be like some that I've seen. Certainly, for that girl's sake, I hope hers proves different. And yet she's started out by letting her husband take her away from everything she's ever known, bringing her here to a land that obviously frightens her. I can't help but think of those poor women of the Earp family, stuck there in Tombstone in near poverty and given no say at all over their own lives, expected to keep house and do the washing and ironing and the cooking and having to leave every single decision to their menfolk. And if Wyatt Earp wants to take his mistress to the most expensive restaurant in town while his wife sits home by herself, she's supposed to accept that, too!''

Dan Stockard was a little startled by her intensity of feeling. He saw her argument, but he felt he had to point out: ''Don't forget, society also requires that the man provide for his wife and give her protection.''

''I know,'' Nellie admitted. ''My trouble is that I've never got in the habit of being protected and provided for!''

''You've been on your own a long time, haven't you?'' he said, remembering what Bart Heywood had told him of her history.

''An awful long time! Since my sister and I lost our parents and came over from Ireland by ourselves. . . .''

There were many things he would have liked to learn— how she had managed to make her way and what circumstances had brought her to this far-western region. But he thought there was much he could read between her words. He could see that she'd discovered freedom on this mining frontier and learned ways a self-reliant young woman could earn an honest living without recourse to the dismal choices usually open to a lone immigrant girl—accepting an undesired marriage or going into domestic service or perhaps on the streets.

It was as though she read his thoughts. ''A body wants something useful to do,'' she said. ''In the camps, there are so many who are far from home, just like me. All those lonely prospectors, living mainly on hope, and the others who risk their lives every day working for pitiful wages down in the mines, with no one to care if they have a decent place to sleep or food to eat, or even if they're killed or injured on the job. But someone *has* to care! More than that, someone has to find the money to help them and their families when they need it.''

Stockard said in quiet admiration, ''It's easy to see why

you're 'the miners' angel.' I don't know anything that fits you better.'' She shook her head with a gesture of denial, but he persisted. ''There must surely have been plenty of men who wanted to marry you. Are you that unwilling to give up your independence? Or is it the right man never came along?''

But he had gone too far. He saw her stiffen, and then her head came up, and there was a warning flash in her eye. ''Sure, and aren't you being a little personal, Mr. Stockard?''

''Afraid I am,'' he admitted. ''Sorry if I've offended you.''

She turned away without answering. But though they walked back to the waiting coach in silence, Dan Stockard sensed that she wasn't really as put out with him as she let on.

A late arrival at Globe meant another night in hotel rooms. After discreet inquiries the next day—a rainy and dismal morning—they went in search of the person they had come such a distance to see. Presently, Stockard found himself being introduced to the woman who might or might not be Doc Holliday's legal wife and who had also been known to Tombstone, variously, as Kate Fisher, Kate Elder, or simply as Big-Nosed Kate.

They sat in the deserted dining room of a sprawling boardinghouse, at one end of a long table from which the remains of breakfast had recently been cleared away. Kate insisted on pouring cups of coffee for all three. She had seemed pleased to greet Nellie and to inquire of the news at Tombstone in the months since she left. But she looked puzzled and suspicious as she said, ''I'm still in the dark about what brings you to Globe, Nellie, and who this gent is that says he wants to see me.'' She looked a direct challenge at the stranger.

Stockard had been studying the woman, judging her to

be about thirty, though she seemed older. She bore the marks of a checkered life, beginning—so Nellie had told him—when she ran away from home in Iowa at the age of sixteen and stowed away on a Mississippi steamboat. She was no beauty, but she had a keen and level blue-eyed stare and a mouth and jaw that invited no nonsense. Curiously enough, despite what she was called, her nose didn't seem a particularly prominent part of her features.

"I won't lie to you," he said bluntly. "I'm a detective. I've been hired to investigate the robberies of silver shipments off the stages out of Tombstone, including the one last March that failed and got your husband into trouble."

He saw how her face froze. "Are you from Wells Fargo?"

"No—an independent. A private party hired me."

"And you brought him here?" Kate exclaimed, turning an accusing stare on the other woman. "Nellie, I wouldn't have believed it of you!"

Nellie Cashman met her look. "I was hoping you wouldn't feel that way. If it was a mistake, I can only say I'm sorry. But surely you must see that lawlessness like that can't be allowed to continue without an attempt, at least, to do something. And I trust this man, or else I wouldn't have brought him to Globe. But so far he's up against a stone wall. If there's anything you'd be able to tell him—"

"I don't know anything. Nothing at all!"

"I think you told the sheriff you did," Dan Stockard pointed out quietly.

She made an impatient gesture. "I signed a paper—and without even reading it. I'd had too much to drink; and, anyway, I was desperate and trying to find a way to get Doc out of Tombstone—shake him loose from them Earps. I guess I had some half-baked notion I could put a scare into him."

"But it didn't work?"

Kate's mouth hardened bitterly. "When I sobered up, I knew all I'd done was end things forever between Doc and me. We'd had fights before, but after that, I figured *I'd* better be the one to get out if I knew what was good for me!"

"Were you really afraid he'd hurt you?" Nellie asked.

"I was afraid he'd *kill* me! I'm still Doc Holliday's woman. Reckon I always will be! After all . . ." Her mouth quirked wryly.

"I set fire to a hotel once to help him get away from the law! I guess it's because I see something in him other people never get to. But when he's drinking, he's a wild man—and he drinks more all the time. It's on account of those bugs in his lungs that are killing him. They make him hate the world—even me sometimes. Still and all, anytime he wants me, back I'll go. But never again to Tombstone!"

"All due to the Earps?" Dan Stockard asked.

There was a note of ferocity in her reply. "That Wyatt Earp has got him wrapped around his little finger! Maybe Doc thinks he sees in him the man he could have been—I don't know. Anyway, there's a streak in Doc's nature: Once he decides to call a man his friend, as far as he's concerned, that man can never do anything wrong. But apparently that don't apply to his woman! Loyalty's fine," she added with a shrug. "But I want him standing on his own two feet, not tagging after somebody with as many enemies as Wyatt Earp! The way things are going, it'll bring him to no good end."

Nellie reminded her, "You've told me the pair of them have terrible arguments."

"Oh, hell, yes—dandies! After the last big one, I was hoping maybe they were gonna bust up for good. But they patched it up, and that's when I finally lost hope."

"When was this?" Stockard asked curiously.

"Back in March. I think it was just a few days after that Benson holdup. I came back to our room and heard them in there really going after it hammer and tongs. But they clammed up the minute I walked in. All I could tell was that it had something to do with Wyatt's disguises.''

"What were those?"

"They were things in a suitcase he used to store with us—for some reason, he didn't want to keep them around his own place. I knew what was in the bag, of course—I'd got curious once and peeked. But that day it was open, with everything strewed all over the bed. And you could almost feel the anger in the room, so thick a knife could cut it. When he seen me, Wyatt dumped everything back in the suitcase and stomped out with it, not saying another word. And Doc went out and got drunker than I ever remember seeing him!''

Dan Stockard felt a stir of excitement. "Tell me more about those disguises.''

"Oh, they were all sorts of junk—the most childish nonsense. It made me wonder if Wyatt Earp was really all that bright! He had one outfit a parson might wear, and there was a straw hat with a checkered suit and cane like would belong to a traveling salesman. Heaven knows what he wanted them for—or the wigs and masks. . . .''

"Masks?"

"Sure. Homemade stuff," the woman said scornfully. "Put together out of odds and ends, with pieces of rope unraveled and pasted on for hair.''

"Something like this?" And Dan Stockard took from his pocket a crude object mine owner Bart Heywood had given him—cut from black cloth, with rope hair and beard attached. He laid it on the table, saying, "I brought it along, meaning to ask if you remembered ever seeing anything like it.''

Kate reached out as though to touch it, then jerked her hand again. "Where did that come from?" she demanded sharply.

"That Benson holdup," Stockard said. "A number of

these things were found on the ground where the bandits left their horses. Wyatt Earp persuaded the sheriff to keep it quiet—he said the masks might be easier to trace if the bandits didn't realize they'd wound up in the hands of the posse. I guess we know now why he *really* wanted it kept secret! And why this clue never led anywhere. . . ."

Nellie Cashman stared at the mask, unspeaking, as Kate Holliday's face drained slowly white.

Later, alone again with Stockard, Nellie asked, "What do you think now? Was it worth the trip?"

"Yes," he stated emphatically. "Even if I'm not sure yet what it all adds up to."

"I'm afraid it's quite obvious, isn't it? At least that thing in your pocket makes it certain Wyatt Earp was in on the holdup."

"Maybe. Or maybe not." He thought it out as he talked. "Doc Holliday was an old friend of Bill Leonard, one of the stage robbers. And Doc has some strange but definite ideas about friendship! If he knew a robbery was being planned and he had a suitcase full of disguises handy, it would have made perfectly good sense to him to lend his friend some of these masks without Wyatt's knowledge. He'd have been fully expecting to get them back, of course. And then, smart enough to guess he might be suspected because of knowing Leonard, he took the trouble of deliberately using Old Man Fuller to establish himself an alibi. But through carelessness the masks were lost, and when Wyatt saw them and realized the danger Doc had put him in, he'd have had every reason to be furious."

"You really think that's what happened? Isn't it a little farfetched?"

"I don't know. I'm only speculating. The other possibility is that *you're* right—that Wyatt's anger was on account of

Doc and his friends messing up an operation Wyatt had planned—losing the masks, killing a couple of men, and then, with all of that, missing their chance at the treasure box. *Is* Wyatt Earp guilty, or isn't he? I still don't know, and I'm beginning to wonder if I ever will!''

Chapter 11

The clouds and rain had passed, giving way to clear October weather with its sunny days and frosty nights. The return from Globe had occurred without incident, and the afternoon following the five-day journey found Dan Stockard again in the saloon at Charleston, sitting in a desultory game of low-stakes stud poker with Ike Clanton, Sid Whelan, and a couple of cowboy hangers-on. The flyblown windowpanes held a dazzle of sunlight and cloudless sky, but the street door had been closed against a seeping chill.

Stockard's attention was mostly on Ike Clanton. He had returned to find Tombstone awash with new rumors, sprung up overnight and centered on the figure of Clanton; and now the man was clearly showing the effect those rumors were having. He had been drinking heavily, and it put him in a surly and belligerent mood, which made the other players edgy as they covertly watched him. There was little talk against the background of noise from a banjo clock on the wall behind the bar and from the dry rattling of newspaper pages in the hands of the bored bartender.

Suddenly, the door was wrenched open, and Frank McLowery burst in. The cocky little rancher had lost something of his swagger. He threw a distracted look around the room, then spotted Ike Clanton and at once came over to the table, the high heels of his boots thumping the floor. While the card players watched, he dropped a hand on Ike's shoulder and leaned to pant a whispered message.

Clanton impatiently shrugged the hand aside. "What's that?" he demanded. "Speak up—I can't hear you."

Repeating, McLowery made no effort now to keep his voice down. "I said Curly Bill and Ringo rode in a minute ago. I think they're looking for us!"

Ike Clanton scowled, absorbing the words through the haze of whiskey he had been drinking. He swore, flung down his cards, and in the same motion scooped his money off the table into a palm. He shoved the money into a pocket as he scraped the legs of his chair back from the table.

No one knew whether he meant to escape or was preparing to go face the men who sought him. The next moment, it was too late for either: The door opened a second time, and Curly Bill Brocius came striding into the saloon with John Ringo at his elbow. They were trailed by three more of the gang, only one of whom—a man named Pony Deal—was personally familiar to Dan Stockard. As they came tramping over to the table where the poker game had by now been completely forgotten, Ike Clanton seemed visibly to brace himself.

It was an indication of the change in Stockard's standing here that no one gave him so much as a look or thought of him as an intruder. This had come about on the day he stepped in and prevented the showdown with the Earps and Doc Holliday, which could have ended disastrously for Ringo and a couple of the gang. Just as Wyatt Earp himself predicted, from that moment on, Stockard had found himself accepted by the Charleston cowboys as though he were almost a member of the gang.

So now he sat back, apparently uninterested but actually

with every sense alert, as Ike Clanton faced the gang leader and Curly Bill said harshly, "So! This is where you been hiding!"

Clanton tried bluster. "Who's hiding? Anybody wanted me, I been right here."

"We want you, all right! What's all this talk around Tombstone about Wyatt Earp and you? And Frank here!" He stabbed a finger at McLowery, who stood by looking acutely ill at ease.

"I dunno who's been filling your head," Ike Clanton muttered sullenly. "But whoever, it's a lie! Every word of it."

"Is that so? You mean Earp never made a deal with you and Frank last summer? It was never arranged that you'd collect the rewards from Wells Fargo for helping bring in the boys who messed up that Benson stage job?"

"No!" The word exploded from Clanton, but it lacked conviction even so. Fear had obviously canceled out the liquor he had been drinking. He was sweating now as he stammered, "Bill Leonard—and Harry Head—and Jim Crane—why, hell! They were friends of ours!"

It was John Ringo who said, too quietly, "And there's nothing lower than the man who'll sell out his friends!"

"From what we heard," Curly Bill said, "you agreed to send word to Bill and the others with plans for another stage job to lure them out of Mexico so Wyatt Earp could bag them. He'd get the credit, and you and Frank would split the two thousand dollars in Wells Fargo reward money on each one. They'd be brought in dead, of course, so no one could ever know who baited the trap."

Frank McLowery exclaimed desperately. "But it never happened!"

"That's right!" Ike eagerly took up the cue. "They all three went and got themselves killed before there would've been time to do anything even if we hadn't told Earp to go to hell with his—''

Johnny Ringo cut him off with a savage cuff to the side of the head. ''Quit lying!''

Jarred by the blow, Ike Clanton almost forgot himself. He cursed and started up from his chair, groping for the gun in his holster. An the last moment, he saw the look on Ringo's face and fell back, breathing hard.

''You don't have to tell us why nothing ever came of the plan,'' Curly Bill Brocius pursued relentlessly. ''It's just too bad for you that after all these months the story went and leaked out!''

Rubbing the side of his head, Ike stammered, ''It was that—that sonofabitch of a Wyatt Earp! Sure he made an offer—and he must've bragged to his friend Williams of the Wells Fargo office that we was in his pocket. But we turned him down! Only thing is, Earp's such a braggart, he never saw fit to tell his friend his big scheme got nixed! Then, night before last, Williams was drinking and called me over to his table to say he knew all about the deal with Earp. I told him there was no deal, but he just kept grinning and saying, far as he was concerned, the thing wouldn't go any farther.''

''Maybe he was too drunk to remember his promise,'' Ringo suggested. ''At any rate, it's all over the county by now!''

Ike Clanton looked sick, his swarthy face beaded with sweat. He looked at his accusers, and suddenly he lurched to his feet and made for the bar, where he picked up a bottle in a trembling hand and looked around for a shot glass. Curly Bill Brocius, with a grimace and a shake of the head, went after him. He took the bottle away from Clanton and set it aside. ''Forget the booze,'' he said sternly, ''and tell us what you mean to do about this!''

''Do?'' Clanton echoed dully, staring at him.

"You and Frank." Curly Bill looked around at Ringo, and with a nod, the latter turned to Frank McLowery, grabbed a handful of his clothing, and hustled him across the room, to slam him up against the bar beside Ike Clanton.

Somewhere or other, Dan Stockard had heard the elder McLowery was considered a dangerous man with a gun, but these two gang leaders showed him little enough respect. Curly Bill looked at him and at Clanton, and he said with icy contempt, "If you expect us to believe for a minute that you never agreed to Earp's deal, you're going to have to do something to prove it. And it had better be something big!"

Clanton rubbed a hand across his mouth. "I—I don't guess I know what you mean."

And Frank McLowery stammered, "What do you call *big*?"

John Ringo had an answer ready for him. "The Earps! Wyatt went too damned far this time. Get him for us—and that town marshal brother of his. Then we'll *know* you won't be making any more deals with them to sell out your friends! Do that and maybe we'll forget this other business."

The two men shared a startled look. "Wyatt? And Virge?" Ike Clanton swallowed. "That's kind of a large order!"

"Well, there it is," Curly Bill said flatly. "Just like Ringo's spelled it out. What's more, we ain't giving you forever, so you better get at it!" He turned away, discouraging any argument. Without another word, he stomped out of the saloon, and after a last meaningful stare, Jonn Ringo followed, leaving a stunned and silent room.

One after another, men pushed back their chairs and went to the bar, and the aproned bartender silently moved around behind to set out glasses and fill them. But they took care to leave a space between themselves and the pair who stood looking as though the roof had fallen in on them.

The poker game was forgotten now. Dan Stockard slowly

let out his breath, then methodically began to gather the scattered cards from around the table and reassemble them into a pack. Beside him, Whelan placed both elbows on the table and said, in a husky voice, "That got kind of rough!"

In the two weeks since he came to this county, none of the cowboys had shown a more complete change of attitude toward Stockard than this Sid Whelan. He seemed a different man from the one who once tried to pull a gun on Stockard and had to be disarmed here in this very saloon. If he'd harbored any resentment over that, it seemed to have been washed out completely on the day in Tombstone when Stockard's quick action prevented Jake Flagg from turning a drunken spree into a disastrous confrontation. Whelan's neck had been among those saved that day, and now the sandy-haired outlaw treated him with respect and a kind of awed admiration. "I sure wouldn't want to be in Ike's boots!" he continued in the same hushed tone. "If I was him or Frank McLowery, I dunno that I'd have any choice right now but to drift!"

"You saying that's what they'll do?"

"Well, it's what *I'd* do. But I'm a drifting man by nature. Ike and Frank, they got ranches to think about. Ain't as easy for them to walk away."

"In that case, it looks like they may have to take on the Earps or else have Brocius and Ringo to answer to. Could be interesting if it happens." Stockard squared up the deck and set it aside. He gave a frowning glance at the banjo clock above the bar. "What time is it, I wonder?" he said suddenly. "That doesn't look as though it could be right."

Whelan dug into a pocket, saying quickly, "Lemme check with—" He broke off, but the silver watch was already in his hand before he realized his mistake. He froze and then slowly lifted his head and met the icy regard of the man beside him. He turned beet red. Then, as Stockard silently held out a hand for it, Whelan laid the watch in his palm.

"That was dumb!" the outlaw grunted sourly. "I forgot just for a minute. But it wasn't me that took it!" he added. "One of the other boys; I'd rather not have to say which one!"

Stockard let him stew while he examined the timepiece. It didn't appear to have suffered any damage. He held it to his ear to make certain it was running. "There was a chain," he reminded Whelan.

The outlaw shook his head. "I never seen it. We played high card, and the other fellow lost. I dunno what he might have done with a chain."

Dan Stockard shrugged and dropped the watch into a pocket of his vest. "We'll forget the chain," he said. No one in the clot of men gathered along the bar seemed to have witnessed the return of his stolen property or heard their low-pitched talk. In the same tone, he demanded, "Which of them was you?"

Whelan started to bridle. "Me? What makes you think—?" But he suddenly dropped the pose and admitted, lifting a shoulder, "I helped hold a gun on the ones in the coach, and then suddenly all hell started to bust loose! That whole operation was a dumb mistake—something we cooked up on the spur of the moment. We should've known there wasn't anything worth having on that stage. . . . And what about it?" he added with a flare of belligerence. "Now that you know, what are you going to do about it?"

Stockard gave him a look of faint surprise. "Why should I do anything? I figure I'm lucky I got my watch back. To tell you the truth," he added, letting a note of disgust into his voice, "this is about the only piece of what I'd call luck that I've seen since I hit this county!" He picked up the depleted handful of coins and bills that was left of his table stakes, looked at it with a rueful shake of the head, and shoved it into a pocket of his coat. "I don't mind saying it isn't too comfortable being this close to the bottom of the barrel!"

He glanced up then and found Whelan looking at him, a peculiar expression in his pale eyes. Whelan said slowly, "You mean it? You need a stake? How particular are you as to where you get it?"

Stockard met the look. "Right now, not very damn particular at all!"

The outlaw's glance dropped suggestively to the opening of Stockard's coat. "What about the gun? I hope you got no objections to using it—"

"I've used it before."

"All right, if you're serious. But give me a little time." Sid Whelan stood up from the table, adding, "You understand, I don't promise nothing."

"Then I've got nothing to lose, have I?" Stockard replied with a shrug.

Chapter 12

For four days after the cowboy leaders gave Ike Clanton and Frank McLowery their ultimatum, matters had been hanging fire; yet to a careful observer like Stockard, it was clear this could not go on indefinitely. Things were bound to come to a head.

At something past noon on the blustery last Wednesday of October, Dan Stockard took his usual route across the fence and the side yard to Bart Heywood's study, where he found the miner in a state of considerable alarm. "What the hell's going *on* out there?" the man blurted, drumming the desk with nervous fingers.

"It could be anybody's guess," Stockard said, "but it does look like things are building for trouble. I almost thought it had come last night. Ike Clanton and Tom McLowery rode into town, and as usual Ike got to drinking and using his mouth, talking about a showdown with the Earp clan."

This had lately become an all-too-familiar pattern. It had really made unnecessary the quiet warning Stockard had passed to Marshal Virgil Earp, after that scene in the saloon at Charleston, that he would do well to be on the lookout. But Clanton's loud talk had been full of inconsistencies—with one breath accusing Wyatt Earp and Doc Holliday of spreading lies about him; with the next, blaming them for spilling the beans and blabbing the details of what had been a sworn, secret agreement.

"Ike Clanton talks a good fight," Stockard pointed out, "though you can wonder if he has the stomach for anything stronger. About midnight, though, Doc Holliday got him in a corner and challenged him to back up his talk. Ike didn't have a gun, so Holliday ordered him to get one. Virgil Earp stepped in and put an end to the business, for the moment at least. But this morning Ike has been out on the town again, carrying a six-gun and a rifle and telling the world that if Holliday and the Earps want a fight, then he and his friends are ready."

"D'you suppose he means it?" Heywood asked.

"Well, he surely has to realize the Earps are trained gunmen, more than a match for anybody that a bunch of part-time rustlers and stage robbers can put against them. But things may have gone just too far—all because that fellow Williams couldn't keep his mouth shut!"

"I've talked to Marsh Williams about that," Heywood said. "He tells me that early last summer Wyatt Earp asked him to wire San Francisco and confirm whether Wells Fargo's rewards for those three stage robbers would be payable either alive or dead. The answer came back 'yes,' and later Williams saw Earp showing the telegram to Clanton and Frank McLowery. He put two and two together and guessed what was afoot.

"But he sat on it all these months, not saying a word to anyone—until one evening he happened to get a little tight and mentioned to Ike what he knew. And now the fat's in the fire, and Marsh blames himself for everything."

"I guess you've got to give some of the blame to Wells Fargo," Stockard commented. "That was a bad business, posting dead-or-alive offers for men who hadn't yet been convicted of anything. But sometimes big companies do things like that. I've never forgotten it was the Pinkertons who exploded a flare in Jesse James's home back in '76 in Missouri—killed his half brother and blew off his mother's arm! It's one of the main reasons I finally decided to quit Pinkerton and try to go it on my own—be responsible for my own mistakes, not have to share the guilt for someone else's."

"If a thing's to be done right," Bart Heywood nodded, "a man better put his own hand to it and take the full responsibility. For quite a while, some of us in this town have been talking about forming a Citizens' Safety Committee. Well, with things looking like they've come to a head, we've gone to work and done it. And right now, unless I'm mistaken, it's about time I called some of our boys together!"

Vigilantes! Dan Stockard thought with cold distaste. But all he said was "I suppose in an emergency there's sense in being ready to back up your law officers."

"The Earps, you mean?" Heywood shrugged. "I suppose we'll have to if it comes to that. But it's the town I'm mostly concerned about. I won't stand by and let them Earps or anyone else turn it into a battleground for their own purposes.

"Because, if you want to know what *I* think," the mine owner went on heavily, "the real reason Wyatt Earp planned to bring those three bandits in dead rather than alive was in order to cover his own tracks. He's just lucky fate took care of the job for him!"

Stockard looked at him sharply. Slowly, he remarked, "It appears to me your mind is pretty much made up. I could almost wonder why you bothered to hire me."

"For *proof*!" Heywood slapped a meaty palm flat on the desk. "Damn it, I need hard evidence I can show Mayor Clum and the others who still insist on taking Wyatt Earp at face value! So far,'' he added pointedly, ''you haven't given me much.''

Dan Stockard thought then of a particular suitcase and its contents belonging to Wyatt Earp and formerly stored in Doc Holliday's room. He could well imagine the conclusion Heywood would jump to if he knew about it—which was the very reason Stockard planned to keep quiet about that piece of information until he himself was fully satisfied what it meant.

Not answering the man's remark, he got to his feet now, picking up his hat. ''I have a feeling I'd better get back to Allen Street in case something does happen.''

''If it happens to Wyatt Earp,'' Bart Heywood pointed out, ''you realize you'll be out of a job. With him dead, it wouldn't matter any longer what he might have been up to.''

Stockard considered that. ''Not to you, perhaps,'' he said finally. ''But once I get started on a trail, I don't much like to quit before I've followed it to the end.''

''Then you may be following it on your own time!''

''We'll see.''

Stockard went across the room and raised the window. When he looked back, Heywood was at a corner cupboard, a bowler hat set aggressively on the back of his head while he took down from its pegs an efficient-looking sawed-off shotgun.

A cold rain the day before had washed the desert sky crisply clear. Lifting on the horizon, the Chiricahua Mountains wore a white mantling of snow that would probably soon vanish. Dan Stockard was still bristling over Bart Heywood's criticisms and talk of vigilantes, either of them a threat to what he was trying to accomplish here. He had suspected the mine owner was a stubborn man, but in his own way, so was Dan Stockard! Having sunk his teeth into a problem, he wasn't easily persuaded to let go.

Just now, though, as he walked along Fremont Street, he found himself caught up in the strange air of waiting excitement that seemed to hold Tombstone in its grasp. And when he reached the corner of First Street, he heard someone call to him in an anxious and tremulous voice.

She stood in the doorway of a small adobe dwelling, wringing her hands and looking almost as though perched for anxious flight. Indeed, there was something birdlike about her, a tiny person in a homemade housedress. She called again, "Mister! Oh, please!" And then she came hurrying over to him. She stammered, and her eyes appeared enormous against her pale cheeks.

"What can I do for you?" he asked.

"I think I know who you are," she told him breathlessly. "Nellie pointed you out to me—Nellie Cashman. She said you're the one who stepped in, week before last, and kept John Ringo and them cowboys from ganging up on my husband." She added in explanation, "He's the marshal. I'm Virgil Earp's wife, Allie. . . ."

Yes, this pert and tiny woman fit nicely Nellie's description of her. Stockard politely touched a finger to his hat brim. "I suppose you could say something along that line happened. It did look like trouble unless somebody took steps to head it off. Though to be perfectly honest, it looked to me your husband could take care of himself."

She made a gesture with one hand. "Whatever . . . I'm mighty glad you did it. Nellie says for certain," she went on, "you're a body that can be trusted." All at once, she reached and clutched his arm. "Oh, please!" Her whole face twisted in a look of anguish. "Can you give me any idea what in the world is going on? I swear I'm scared half to death!"

Hedging, Stockard asked, "What makes you think anything's going on?"

She shook her head impatiently. "It's plain as day! A little while ago Wyatt—my brother-in-law—he come and got Virge out of bed. Virge had been on night duty, and normally he wouldn't be getting up yet. But from the way they talked, I could tell there was trouble. I heard Wyatt mention something about Ike Clanton. Then Virge put on his gun and went away with him, looking awful grim and not even saying a word when I wanted to fix him some breakfast. And then . . ." Her mouth began to tremble. "A little while ago, one of them loudmouths that always looks for a chance to make a person feel terrible saw me out on the porch, and goin' by, he yelled at me, 'Miz Earp, you'll be a widow by nightfall!' And he *laughed*!"

Dan Stockard's jaw hardened. "A man like that deserves to be shot!" he muttered savagely, then added, "I'm afraid it's true, ma'am, that Ike Clanton is in town and making talk against the Earps. Still, Ike's pretty good at talking, and it doesn't necessarily mean anything will come of it." He placed a reassuring hand on her shoulder. "You'd best stay here, Mrs. Earp. I'll check things out for you. But I wouldn't worry too much just because of a man like Clanton."

"I can't help it!" she cried out, her words a moan of anguish. "I've got an awful bad feeling. . . ."

Stockard patted her shoulder. "I'll see what I can find out," he said, taking his leave.

When he had gone, Allie stood a moment watching him hurry away along Fremont Street. With a shudder of fear, she pulled tight the shawl that she had tossed about her shoulders against the chill of the October day and started back toward the house. But she only took a step or two; blindly, she turned again to stand at the gate, waiting, seeing nothing, but listening—for what, she could not have said.

It seemed an age. Then, suddenly, somewhere down this very street, the shooting began. She cried out and gripped the gatepost with a trembling hand as the sound of gunfire shocked the stillness of the afternoon. The shots tumbled one over another. They seemed to go on and on, endlessly.

Sheriff Johnny Behan was to say later that his initial hint of serious trouble came while he was stretched out in a barber chair with a towel spread over him and the lather being razored from his face. Someone stationed at the window, where he could watch activity in the street, sang out, "The Earps are all over there at Hafford's saloon—just standing around, sort of. Like they're waiting for the show to start."

And the barber himself observed to the room at large, "You ask me, it sure can't be long now."

"What can't?" Johnny Behan demanded with what he claimed was his first real twinge of alarm. "What are you talking about?"

"Why, ain't you heard?" the first man exclaimed. "About how the Earps are building to a showdown with Ike Clanton and the McLowerys? Less than an hour ago, they jumped Clanton and the marshal pistol-whipped him and dragged him into day court and got him fined for carrying a gun in the city limits. Well, now, we all know it's a law, but nobody could enforce it without arresting half the town! They was just picking on Ike.

"A fellow who was there says Clanton sat with his head bleeding and the Earps all around him and swore he'd fight any or all of 'em, anytime. 'Just give me four feet of ground to stand on,' he says. Sure, he's mostly talk; but sooner or later he just might talk himself into a corner where he'll *have* to fight!"

Another customer put in, "Right afterward, Wyatt Earp walked out of the courtroom and bumped into Tom McLowery. The two of them had words, and Wyatt slapped Tom in the face and hit *him* with a gun and laid him in the street, then walked away and left him lying there. Then, a little later, when Tom, Frank McLowery, and Billy Clanton was at the gun shop loading up their shell belts with cartridges, Wyatt come and jumped Frank for his horse being on the sidewalk. They say it looked like he was just daring them to start the ball right then and there, but nothing happened—yet!"

"Bad blood there," the barber said, shaking his head. "I'd say some of it could get spilled before the day's out."

Johnny Behan felt a sick knot of concern forming in his belly. Ike Clanton and his friends were no match for the Earps, and they should know it. There was no way this could be anything but bad news, and suddenly Behan felt as though he was strapped down and helpless under the towel fastened around his neck. All at once his appearance, normally a prime consideration for a man of his personal vanity, didn't seem to matter overmuch. "Hurry it up!" he told the man with the razor. "Get finished and let me up from here!"

It was the fastest shave he ever had, and his face was sore and tingling as he hurried out of the barbershop and across the street to Hafford's, on the corner of Fourth and Allen.

It was easy to see something was afoot from the unusual number of idlers standing about on the sidewalk and even in the street. A murmur of talk rose. Coming nearer, Behan could see a number of men he knew to belong to the self-appointed vigilance committee, an outfit the sheriff looked on with distrust. They were a town organization, after all, backers of the town government and potentially hostile to the county machine of which Sheriff Behan was part.

Then he spotted the Earps—Wyatt and Virge and Morgan—who tended to stand out because of their size and because of the way they dressed alike in the somber black of professional gamblers. All three were armed, and he saw that the marshal had a double-barreled shotgun that he held out in one hand, unobtrusively, its shining tubes pointing alongside one leg to the ground.

Johnny Behan's mouth hardened as he looked on Wyatt Earp, his rival and bitterest enemy. And, of course, there was that creepy little killer Doc Holliday, wearing a long gray overcoat against the chill of the day and leaning his emaciated shape upon a cane, a sure sign that his disease-riddled lungs were giving him particular trouble. When that happened, you could count on it: His mood would be blacker and more dangerous than usual.

Behan passed up the rest and made directly for the marshal. He halted in front of Virgil Earp and demanded, "What's going on?"

Cold eyes surveyed him. Virgil said, almost indifferently, "We got some sons of bitches in town that think they want a fight!"

"What do you mean to do about it?" At what he read in the look the tall man gave him, Johnny Behan's eyes widened. Aghast, he cried, "You're the marshal! You can't—"

"I'm giving them a choice!" Virgil Earp snapped back at him. "They'll let themselves be arrested and go to jail—or far as I'm concerned they can have their fight! I don't give too much of a damn which they choose. I'm through fooling with them!"

The sheriff gnawed at his lip in an agony of debate. "I'll go talk to them," he declared suddenly. "Where are they now?"

Earp made a careless gesture with the barrel of the

shotgun. "Around the corner," he said. "On Fremont—in that vacant lot west of Fly's, somebody said. But this thing has gone on too long already," he reminded the sheriff dangerously.

"You'll wait till I come back!" Johnny Behan said grimly, and started away.

A stinging gust of wind whipped grit from the street about his legs as the sheriff started up Fourth Street, aware of a hundred curious eyes that followed him—aware, too, that it was a perilous game he was playing. If he could defuse this situation and prevent the explosion the whole town was expecting, it would be a political triumph for the sheriff's office and give him a tremendous advantage over the Earps. But should he try and fail, then whatever else came of it, Johnny Behan would be the certain loser.

Behan's nerves were raw and his temper short when he reached the corner of Fremont and discovered Frank McLowery standing there holding his horse by the reins, peering down toward the crowd at Hafford's. The sheriff exclaimed angrily, "Frank! What the hell do you think you're up to?"

"Keeping an eye on those bastards. Making sure they don't get a drop on us. . . ."

"Who's with you?"

"My brother Tom . . . Ike and Billy Clanton."

And glancing along the south side of Fremont toward Third Street, Behan could indeed see the little knot of men gathered at an empty lot near the far end of the block. He let out his breath. "Come along," he said shortly. "I want to talk to all of you."

Here, more eyes were watching, from doorways and windows and from the boardwalk on the opposite side of the street. All Tombstone seemed to be holding its breath, waiting to see what would happen—waiting to see how Sheriff Behan would cope. With McLowery leading his animal, they walked west together along the street, past the Papago Cash Store, past the rear entrance to the O.K. Corral, past Bauer's meat market with its awning, and past the two buildings, front and rear, that housed Camillus Fly's photographic gallery and lodging house.

If Behan had wondered just what Ike Clanton and the others were up to, loitering in the open area that separated Fly's from a couple of buildings on the corner of Third Street, he understood when he saw the wink of sunlight on glass as one of them tilted a whiskey bottle to his mouth and then passed it on. Pouring courage down their throats—getting primed.

Behan sorted them out: Ike Clanton, his head bandaged from the blow of Virgil Earp's six-gun; Ike's tough eighteen-year-old brother, Billy; Tom McLowery, a youngster about the same age. There was a fifth one, along with the McLowery and Clanton brothers—a fellow named Billy Claiborne whom Johnny Behan dismissed as a swaggering nonentity despite the pair of pistols he sported. In the background, where he seemed to be doing little more than looking on, he also spotted Wes Fuller, son of the old man who hauled the water wagon from the San Pedro. He probably didn't count, either.

"Boys, hasn't this gone far enough?" the sheriff asked the Clantons and McLowerys. "Somebody's going to end up getting hurt!" he added as persuasively as he could manage.

"What do you call what they already done to my brother Tom? And to Ike?" Frank McLowery replied harshly; he seemed to be the aggressive one here. "There's nothing more humiliating than to lay a gun barrel over a man's skull!"

Behan had to agree. "There was no call for that, I admit."

"So what do you expect us to do? Roll over and play dead? Let them Earps tromp all over us?"

"I want you to give me your guns. You boys know where my office is. Go turn your weapons in and wait there for me."

"Like hell!" Frank McLowery said, his voice fairly trembling now. "Not while them bastards still got theirs! All right, so Virge is the marshal. None of the rest have any such excuse, yet they're walking around armed to the teeth! Go take *their* guns. Until then, you or nobody else is going to get mine!" And he dropped his hand to the butt of his holstered six-shooter.

Johnny Behan hesitated. Despite the chill of the afternoon, he felt a run of sweat break and trickle down over his ribs. This wasn't going well at all. He hadn't really thought they would defy him. These were his friends; more importantly, they were his constituents. It was the vote of ranchers like these—the men of the county who opposed the Tombstone town machine—that he had to depend on to keep him in office. He knew he must preserve the peace but wasn't about to treat them like criminals just because the Earps were involved.

He appealed to the elder Clanton. "What do *you* say, Ike?"

The latter shook his head. "I'm clean, Johnny. They took my guns when they arrested me. You can look and see I ain't armed."

And, in fact, he stood and let the sheriff run his hands about his waist, satisfying himself that indeed the man had no weapon on him. Behan looked at Tom McLowery, who said quickly, "Me, either," and spread open the skirts of his coat for the sheriff's inspection. "I checked my gun and rifle with Andy Mehan at his saloon—like the law says."

Behan ran the back of a fist across his jaw, which was still tender from the hurried scrape of the barber's razor. "How about you, Claiborne?"

"You don't need my guns. Or Billy Clanton's, either. We ain't in this. We was just fixing to pull out of town."

So there it stood, and as far as the sheriff could see, he had accomplished nothing. While he debated what he would go back and tell Virgil Earp, there was a sudden exclamation from someone, and he turned. What he saw filled him with alarm.

The Earps hadn't waited. They had just turned the corner onto Fremont, and they approached now along the sidewalk, their boots knocking back a solid run of sound from the dry planks. Johnny Behan bit back a groan of frustration. "You stay here!" he told the others. And then he hurried off to meet the advancing men.

Doc Holliday was with them, bringing up the rear with Morgan, while Wyatt and Virgil walked in front. All of them wore holsters; Wyatt Earp's pistol was openly in his hand. A sudden gust of wind plucked aside the long tail of Holliday's coat, and Behan glimpsed the shining barrels of the shotgun he carried alongside his leg. It was the same shotgun Virgil had been holding earlier. Apparently, they had traded, for now the marshal had Doc's cane in his own right hand. They came on like that—four tall men, coming two by two, deliberate and without haste.

Johnny Behan met them under the awning of Bauer's market, just east of Fly's. "Don't go down there!" he cried, trying to block their way. And in desperation, because it was the last thing he could think of that might stop this, he said, "It's all right, I took their guns."

Hearing that and apparently believing it, Wyatt Earp slid his own pistol into a pocket of his long coat, but he kept his hand on it. But the marshal's gray eyes, studying Behan, were skeptical.

"Did you arrest them?" Virgil Earp asked. Behan hesitated, but he could only shake his head. "Then get out of our way!'' Virgil said curtly, and the sheriff found himself pushed aside.

"No!" He started after them, protesting. "Damn it, I'm the sheriff of this county. I'm ordering you to stop!" They paid no more attention than they might to the yapping of a terrier. And as Johnny Behan followed helplessly in their wake, unheard and unheeded, someone called eagerly into the windy silence, *"Here they come!"*

Chapter 13

"**H**ere they come!"

The yell from outside penetrated the quiet of the front room at Camillus Fly's, a room converted with drapes, props, lights, and equipment into a studio for portrait photography. It interrupted Nellie Cashman as she was discussing the publicity picture she had in mind for her own place of business, the Russ House. She had felt the bearded Mr. Fly was only politely trying to pay attention, having his mind elsewhere; now, with a muttered exclamation, he proved it as he strode past her to the street door and threw it open.

Beyond the photographer's stocky figure, Nellie caught a glimpse of several men going by on the wooden sidewalk at a slow but deliberate pace. They were soon out of sight, but something in the look of them drew Nellie Cashman, like a magnet, to a side window that let in the bleak sunlight of midafternoon.

Here she had a view of the open space between this building and an assay office adjoining it on the west. Earlier, she'd noticed some men idling there and passing a bottle around. She saw they were there still. Some fifteen feet separated the buildings, with Fremont on her right and an alley to her left, beyond which were the open stalls of the O.K. Corral. The men were no longer drinking;

they were standing roughly in a line with their backs against the adobe wall of the assay office.

Nellie, who had a good memory for faces, thought she recognized the rancher, Frank McLowery, next to the street and holding his horse by the reins, with his taller, younger brother Tom at his right elbow and Billy and Ike Clanton just beyond. She saw Wes Fuller and another man who was a stranger to her, but they seemed to be backing away as though they no longer wanted to be any part of this group.

Then she saw the Earps.

They came once more into her range of view—three tall men in their somber black garb, and a fourth who was the consumptive and, to Nellie, rather sinister Doc Holliday. They had been two abreast as they passed the door of the photography studio. Now they were spread out, elbow to elbow, as they entered the narrow yard where the Clantons and McLowerys waited. As though at a signal, Wes Fuller and the other one—whose name she would learn later was Billy Claiborne—turned and lit out at a run, putting distance between themselves and what was about to take place.

The newcomers halted, no more than a couple of yards separating the two lines and in such a position that the solid figures of the Earps nearly blocked Nellie's view of the others. But she saw the gesture when Virgil Earp lifted the cane he was carrying. And she heard the marshal say into the stillness, "You men put up your hands! I want your guns!"

Someone yelled a curse. Nellie didn't see who it was that fired the opening shots. Recoiling, she spun away from the window as both hands flew to her face in horror and revulsion.

Dan Stockard, approaching from the west, had held up at the Third Street intersection when he caught sight of Doc Holliday and the Earps a block ahead of him. They were talking to the sheriff, Johnny Behan; he saw angry gestures but could hear nothing of what was being said. But in the next moment, Virgil Earp impatiently brushed Behan aside, and then the somber-clad quartet came on at a swift and purposeful stride. And from their manner, Stockard knew that events were very near to breaking.

The attention of the Earps appeared to be centered on an open lot that was hidden from Stockard by a pair of corner buildings. They had been moving by twos along the sidewalk, but now he saw how Doc and Morgan shifted into line with the others as they all pivoted to enter that area, four abreast. In an effort to keep his eyes on them, Stockard circled hastily into the street. Over on the farther sidewalk, he saw some people collected and intently staring across in the direction of the photographer's studio.

He barely had time to join them. Just as he reached Addie Bourland's Millinery, he heard a gunshot across the street and another on the heels of it; he whirled about to glimpse the two groups of men who stood confronted now in the vacant lot next to Fly's. He was just in time to see Frank McLowery start to double forward, a hand clutched to his belly. And with that the gunfire became general, flat reports that mingled and echoed off the sounding boards of wooden siding and adobe while smoke from exploding cartridges built into a streaking cloud.

Still holding his gun, Frank McLowery was stumbling and weaving as he staggered across the sidewalk and out into the street; the Earps let him go, apparently convinced he was out of the fight. An instant later, Billy Clanton was hit. Stockard saw him thrown hard against the adobe wall at his back, to go sliding down it. His gun arm seemed badly injured, but as he sat there in the dust, Stockard saw him fumbling and trying to take the pistol in his other hand. And now Ike Clanton was running forward, straight toward his enemies. He grabbed for Wyatt Earp and pawed frantically at him as he yelled in a voice on the edge of hysteria, "Don't shoot me! I ain't got a gun!"

Wyatt flung the man off. His shouted answer held utter contempt. "This thing has started! Either get to fighting or get away!" For just an instant, Clanton stood in an agony of indecision. After that, he turned and scampered toward Fly's and along the side of the building, to vanish around a rear corner. Someone in the Earp party hurried him with a couple of bullets, flung too hastily to do him any damage.

The fight was moving away from the vacant lot now, into the street and out of the blinding fog of powder smoke. Frank McLowery was somehow still on his feet despite the shock of the bullet he had taken. Now Stockard caught sight of Tom as the younger McLowery ducked for protection behind a horse that had been left standing half across the sidewalk on trailing reins. At that very moment, a bullet must have stung the animal's rump, for it tossed its head and bolted wildly.

Stockard couldn't see any gun in the young fellow's hand, but as the horse went by him, he made a desperate lunge for the rifle in its saddle. His attempt failed. He stumbled back empty-handed, and as he stood exposed, Doc Holliday brought up a double-barreled shotgun that must have been hidden under the skirt of his long coat. It blasted, spurting smoke. At that point-blank range, the entire load of buckshot found its mark. Tom McLowery took the full force of it and was sent reeling around the corner of the assay office, to go staggering along the sidewalk toward Third Street, probably dying on his feet.

One of the Earps was suddenly down, out in the street, but he climbed to his feet again; it was Morgan. Frank McLowery stood brace-legged in the middle of Fremont shouting something at Doc Holliday, who now tossed aside his empty shotgun and pulled a revolver. He and Morgan both fired at McLowery, knocking him to the ground even as he was triggering a shot at Holliday. Though Stockard might have been mistaken, he thought he saw Doc Holliday stagger and catch his footing in the street ruts, very much as though he had been hit.

All at once, the fight seemed to be over. The guns fell silent; there was a stillness almost deafening after the continuous racket of gunfire. But even yet, Billy Clanton wasn't ready to quit. He was young, and he was tough. He crawled painfully through the dust and weeds toward his enemies, dragging himself along with what was left of his strength. Somehow he brought his revolver wavering up and tried a last shot at Virgil Earp. The marshal was hit; he staggered but didn't fall. In the next breath, Morgan and Wyatt, firing together, put two bullets into Billy Clanton, and he dropped back, limp.

The battle, which seemed endless, had actually lasted something under thirty seconds. It had left the Earps and Doc Holliday still on their feet with all their opponents dead or routed—but, incredibly, Billy Clanton was still not through! Sprawled on the sidewalk, looking more dead than alive and bleeding from half a dozen wounds, he was trying gamely to raise his smoking gun. In front of the photography studio, a man Stockard took to be Camillus Fly himself was shouting, "Somebody take that damn thing away from him!"

Someone yelled back, "Take it away from him yourself!"

The photographer swore, but he hurried across the open lot, where streaks of dust and smoke were only now beginning to unravel and disperse, and leaned to remove the smoking gun from Billy Clanton's fingers. The boy hadn't strength left to resist. He shook his head in protest and appeared to mumble something, but he let the weapon go.

The scene was beginning to fill with the curious, who

had watched from a safe distance or were only belatedly reaching the scene of the brief but deadly shoot-out. Wyatt Earp loomed tall among them. The only one of the clan to come through completely unscratched, he went now to look to the condition of the others. A crowd was gathering about Virgil, who had let himself down to a seat on the edge of the boardwalk, right leg extended stiffly before him. Morgan swayed uncertainly, with blood beginning to show on the upper part of his body. Yonder, Doc Holliday stood apart with an aloof and dangerous attitude that seemed to dare anyone to come near him. If he had been wounded in the fight, he gave no hint of it.

By now, Dan Stockard had joined the crowd milling in confusion about the scene of the battle. Elbowing a way for himself, he heard a medley of talk that was part eyewitness reporting and part wild speculation. He was in time to see Sheriff Behan approach Wyatt Earp and hear him declare loudly, "I'm putting you under arrest for murder!"

The slate-gray eyes, frigid with anger, met Behan's. "Not today, you aren't!" Wyatt Earp retorted. "Damn you, you lied to us! You said they'd been disarmed!"

Johnny Behan tried an answer, but it seemed to get lost somewhere before it reached his tongue. And Earp simply turned his back on him.

A doctor had arrived to make quick examination of the carnage. Frank McLowery, crumpled in the dirt of the street, was obviously dead. Billy Clanton, bullet riddled, still clung to life, but with all the damage that had been done to him, it was clear he would not last long. The doctor administered a shot of morphine and gave orders for volunteers to lift and carry him beyond the assay office to a private dwelling at the corner of Third Street.

On that same corner, still another body lay crumpled at the foot of a telegraph pole. Young Tom McLowery, carrying a fatal load of buckshot from Doc Holliday's shotgun, had managed to stagger that far before collapsing there to die. After no more than a glance, the doctor turned his attention to the ones who could still get some benefit from it: Morgan, with a bullet in his shoulder, and Virgil, who had taken one through the calf of his right leg. Doc Holliday stood aloof and unapproachable; he could hardly be seriously hurt, if at all.

Suddenly, Allie was there. She came running through the crowd, her eyes wild, her hair tangled. Dan Stockard got to her, and she clutched at him. "My husband! Oh, my God! Is Virgil—?"

"He was hit in the leg," Stockard said. "Maybe not too seriously."

She cried out. Holding her firmly by one arm, Dan Stockard proceeded to clear a way for her among the clot of men gathered where Virgil Earp sat having his wound tended to. "Here's the marshal's wife," Stockard told them. "Give her room, will you?" Allie was crying, close to hysteria as she dropped down in the dust and put her arms about her husband.

There were new arrivals—a dozen grim-faced men who carried rifles and shotguns and immediately took charge. When he saw Bart Heywood and Mayor Clum, Stockard guessed these must be the self-styled Citizens' Safety Committee—the vigilantes, formed in expectation of just such an emergency as the one that had struck Tombstone today. Most set to work restoring order and keeping the crowd back from the injured, but Heywood had something else on his mind. He turned to the mayor and exclaimed, "I want you to relieve Virgil Earp of that marshal's badge, John. If you don't, I'll tear it off his coat myself! He's disgraced the office he was appointed to!"

"Cool off, Bart," John Clum told him. "I promise you, the whole affair is going to be investigated. But this is no time for hasty judgments. Right now, I want a rig fetched so these men can be taken home where their wives can look after them. And I want a guard for them—just in case some hothead takes a mind to square the tables for the ones that are dead and dying.''

Dan Stockard didn't wait to hear more of Heywood's grumbling. He had caught sight of Nellie Cashman standing tremulously on the porch of Fly's gallery, and he hurried to her. Seeing her stricken look, he exclaimed, ''I hope you didn't see that!''

''No.'' She closed her eyes with a shudder. ''I couldn't watch!''

''Thank God. It's over now, though I don't think we've heard the end of it. But there's nothing you or I can do. Let me take you away from here.''

''Oh, yes!'' she agreed faintly. ''Anywhere at all. Anywhere—away from here. . . .''

The place they chose was the kitchen of the Russ House, rich with the aromas of fresh-baked bread and a stew pot simmering on the back of the stove, and just now a neat and quiet oasis amid the fever of excitement that gripped Tombstone. Here Dan Stockard made Nellie take a place at the oilcloth-covered table while he poured coffee for both, laced from a bottle of whiskey he discovered in one of the cabinets— property, he supposed, of the cook. He sat beside her at the table as they talked quietly, and at his request Nellie related everything she had seen and heard in the vacant lot west of Fly's, just north of the O.K. Corral.

''I'm truly relieved,'' he said finally, ''that you didn't watch the fight after it started. I wouldn't want to think of you being involved in any way, not even as a witness.''

''A witness?'' she echoed. ''You think this could go to a court trial?''

"We can count on it. The Earps have powerful enemies. They won't miss a chance to try and discredit them, including hauling them up for murder!"

Stockard got restlessly to his feet. At the window, he stood busy with his thoughts as he looked out upon the blustery afternoon. He heard Nellie ask, "What about yourself, Dan? *You* were a witness."

"Yes, and if it's necessary, I'm ready to come forward and tell as much as I know. I just hope it doesn't come to that. I've worked too hard trying to give certain people an impression that I'm no friend of the Earps. And after all, I didn't even see the start of the fight; I have no idea who actually let off the first shots."

"Neither do I. It all happened so fast—I just couldn't bear to look!"

"One thing I'm sure of—whatever might happen in a courtroom isn't apt to settle anything. The Earps won their fight today, but their enemies will never let it rest there. In fact, we may have seen the beginning of the end for them here in Tombstone. The town leaders have only tolerated and supported them after a fashion as long as they were useful, but they may start turning their backs now that the Earps are in trouble. At the very least, Virgil Earp is bound to have his town marshal's badge taken from him, and once that happens, it will make them fair game for anybody! If you want my opinion, I'm not even sure all of those brothers are going to get out of Tombstone alive!"

She stared at him. "You really think it could come to that? Oh, those poor women!"

At once, he was again at her side, saying earnestly, "I know how you feel about your friends, and I know it's in your nature to want to do whatever you can to help. But please, Nell! Promise you'll be careful about getting mixed up in this! I still have a job to finish here, and it's not going to be any easier with *you* to worry about. I'm being selfish because—believe me, if anything should happen to you . . ."

The dark eyes so near his own went wide in astonishment. Her cheeks flushed. "Why Dan," she whispered in the broadest of Irish brogues. "Sure, and would you be meaning what it sounds like you do?"

Dan Stockard answered with his eyes as he took her elbows and lifted her to her feet. They stood together like that for a long and wondering moment. And then her arms opened to him, and he pulled her close and took the kiss that awaited him on her softly parted lips.

Chapter 14

For a few hours after the deadly street battle, which already, and incorrectly, was being called the "gunfight at the O.K. Corral," an unreasoning panic had swept Tombstone. Steam whistles at the Tough Nut, the Lucky Cuss, and the other Tombstone mines blew the alarm; the day shifts came piling up from underground to learn what was happening. And without knowing quite how, everyone suddenly seemed convinced the long-smoldering feud between the town and the county would now break into the open—that in retaliation for the killings, the tough ranchers of the San Pedro and their friends, the rustlers and gunmen and outlaws, were about to descend on this upstart community.

Wild rumor said they meant to burn Tombstone to the ground, as last summer's four-block blaze had failed to do so. Soon the Citizens' Safety Committee—openly called vigilantes, or even by the crude name of *stranglers*—were out in force patrolling the streets, armed and ready for trouble. A townsman who liked to dress, for greater comfort, in cowman's garb soon found it wise to go home and change to the protection of a suit coat, string tie, and bowler.

But hours passed, and the fears never materialized. Finally, the first shock waves died, and the aftereffects of the shooting slowly set in.

In three of the finest coffins available from the undertaking firm of A. J. Ritter, the bodies of the McLowerys and Billy Clanton lay on exhibit in a storefront window under a banner bearing the words *Murdered on the streets of Tombstone*. Meanwhile, in an adobe over near the Mexican quarter, Virgil and Morgan Earp lay side by side in one bed with their weapons handy and an armed patrol of vigilantes on guard. Virgil was reported recovering well enough from a bullet-skewered leg, but Morgan suffered with his neck and shoulder wound—the slug from Billy Clanton's six-gun had chipped a vertebra.

Dan Stockard understood that Sheriff Behan, stung by the charge that he had lied and let the Earps go to meet their enemies thinking they were all disarmed, had paid a call on Virgil in an attempt to squirm out of that problem. He hadn't quite made himself clear, he said. He had *tried* to disarm Frank McLowery and Billy Clanton but didn't have time. What he had *meant* to say was that he was in the process of disarming them in a last-ditch attempt to avoid a gunfight at whatever cost.

Now, on a bright October afternoon two days after the shooting, Stockard stood in a crowd that lined Allen Street to watch a funeral cortege make its way in the direction of Boot Hill. It was rather more like a circus parade, he thought sourly. Sunlight winked from polished instruments as a brass band marched by, its raucous tones running abrasively under the cloudless and windy sky. Behind came a pair of hearses, all glass and dark wood and somber upholstery, the first one bearing Billy Clanton's coffin, with both the McLowery brothers in the second. And, once more, the banner with its message: *Murdered on the streets of Tombstone*.

The crowd stood packed and silent, ominously watching

the procession go by. Sentiment, which had been running strongly in favor of the marshal and his brothers immediately after the fight, was beginning to turn under a barrage of propaganda from friends of the men they had killed and in the columns of one of Tombstone's two newspapers; for as a rival to Mayor Clum's *Epitaph* and as a chief prop of the county machine, the *Nugget* could be depended on to take a hostile position toward Sheriff Behan's enemies, the Earps. Meanwhile, a coroner's jury had been summoned and heard the evidence and, without either exonerating or condemning, had returned a verdict that Clanton and the McLowerys had met their deaths at the hands of the Earps and one Holliday, known as Doc. And so the pot continued to simmer. . . .

Stockard felt a hand slip into his own. He turned quickly and with pleasure saw that Nellie had joined him. Neither spoke; from the moment of their embrace in the quiet of the Russ House, they were finding, more and more, that mere words weren't always needed. Stockard gave a nod and a quick smile, caught her arm up into the bend of his elbow, and drew her closer. Nellie didn't return the smile. Her lovely face was somber as she gave her attention once more to the crowd and to the procession in the street. She exclaimed, in disapproval, ''Sure, and you'd think it was a picnic or something!''

''The enemies of the Earps are beginning to feel their oats,'' Stockard told her. ''I suppose you know that the mayor finally had to call on Virgil and strip him of his marshal's badge and suspend him from office. I understand Sheriff Behan and Ike Clanton right now are in the process of swearing warrants on a charge of murder!'' He added solemnly, ''I told you that shoot-out was only the beginning—it wasn't the end of anything.''

''Then where *does* it end?'' she exclaimed.

Stockard didn't answer because he only half heard the

question. He had caught sight of a face in the jam of specta-
tors; pale eyes that blinked behind sandy lashes were peering
at him, and now Sid Whelan was elbowing his way purposefully forward. Sidling near enough that Stockard could catch
the smell of whiskey on him, Sid looked uncertainly at the
woman before asking in a low voice, "What we was talking
about, the other day—you still interested?"

Dan Stockard gave a brief nod. "Why not?"

The man didn't like the way Nellie was obviously listening. He gave her a shifty-eyed scowl before he shrugged and
said gruffly, "Hang on, then. I maybe have something on the
fire." Abruptly, he turned and at once was lost in the crowd,
which was breaking up now as the procession with the two
hearses moved slowly on along Allen Street.

Turning to walk with Nellie back toward the Russ House,
Stockard had no inclination to explain that brief exchange
with Sid Whelan. But she was frowning at him intently, and
now she inquired, "Who was that person? What in the world
was he talking about?"

"Probably nothing," he answered briefly. "It'll be best
if you forget it."

"I didn't like him. I didn't like anything about him!"
Her hand tugged at his arm so that Stockard was forced to
halt and meet her expression of grave concern. "Are you
getting into danger of some sort?"

"What makes you think that?" But his attempt to pass it
off missed the mark.

"I worry about you, Dan," she admitted, unmindful of
the flow of traffic around them.

"It's Dave," he whispered. "You must remember that."
Stockard looked quickly about and spied a secluded corner
beside one of the buildings. He covered her hand with his and
led her from the street. As the crowd surged past, now but a
distant and faceless stream, Dan and Nellie stood in the

shadow of the building and sought each other's eyes.

There was no way that things could ever be the same between these two, not after that moment in the kitchen when their arms and lips had met without a hint of warning. Dan Stockard had known women, but none that had ever taken so complete and profound a hold on him. As for Nellie, he thought she seemed almost frightened by the depth of feeling she had suddenly discovered in herself. It filled him with an awed protectiveness toward this young woman—a woman he knew to be thoroughly capable of looking out for herself.

He said earnestly, "You must never worry about me, Nell! That's the first lesson you have to learn. This is my job. I've taken it on, and I have to finish it whatever way I can."

For a moment, she didn't answer. Then it was to say, reluctantly, "You want me to be honest? I'm afraid I don't much care for your job! You'll be using that, I suppose?" She indicated the hidden gun in its clip holster beneath his coat.

"If I have to—I have before. . . . I know you don't think much of guns."

She shuddered in recollection. "How could you expect me to—after what happened the other day outside Fly's studio? And just now, watching that procession on its way to Boot Hill! I've spent too many hours fighting to save life. You can't expect me to enjoy seeing it snuffed out by some man with a gun in his fist!"

He felt a small sting of anger. "I like to see lives saved, too," he answered a little too sharply. "I won't balk at snuffing out vermin if there isn't any other way!"

They stared at each other, an ominous flash of hostility bristling and separating them. Suddenly, appalled and remorseful, Stockard exclaimed, "I'm sorry, Nell! Truth is, I think we're both tied in knots over what's been going on these few days. I know exactly what you meant just now.

Believe me, if only for your sake, I wish there was never any need to use a weapon. But in this country—'' He shook his head.

Her fingers tightened on his. "I think I understand," she said simply. "And—please! Don't let us quarrel over anything. Not *us*!" They stood a moment longer in silence, then turned and walked back out into the street.

Sheriff Behan's warrants were served, but only on Wyatt and Doc Holliday, since Virgil and Morgan were still laid up with their wounds and unable to appear in court. Wells Spicer, the justice of the peace, first set bail at fifty thousand dollars apiece, then was persuaded to reduce this to a manageable ten thousand, which was promptly put up by local businessmen, and the two prisoners were released. And five days after the killings, a formal hearing commenced to determine if charges against the two men should go to the grand jury.

Tombstone was angry and disappointed when Judge Spicer ordered the sessions be held in closed court; obviously, he feared the high feelings on both sides and the repercussions that could result from a public hearing. So the town and the county had to stand by and fume, dependent on rumor and on such news as the daily papers reported. Each day, Stockard read the columns of testimony as eagerly as anyone else.

First, of course, a parade of prosecution witnesses took the stand to depict the killings as inexcusable and wanton murder. A saloonkeeper brought in a gun that he swore Tom McLowery had left with him before the battle. A woman who had been a customer in Bauer's meat market said that as the marshal and his group tramped purposefully by on their way to Fly's, she had heard one say, "Let's get them," and Doc Holliday answer, "That's right!" There were men who claimed to have seen the victims with their hands in the air even as they were being shot. Sheriff Behan himself took the stand to testify that both Tom McLowery and Ike Clanton were weaponless and that he'd heard Billy Clanton begging, "Don't shoot me! I don't want to fight anybody!" Afterward, Billy Claiborne and Wes Fuller came on and swore to hearing exactly the same words.

Dan Stockard got a commentary on that last evidence from none other than Old Man Fuller himself. Stockard found him at the bar of the Alhambra, brooding over a half-emptied glass of beer. Without preamble, the old fellow asked bitterly, "You see what that no-good brat of mine got up and told the judge? Why hell! He'd say any damn thing Ike Clanton or that crowd was to tell him to!"

"He was there, after all," Stockard pointed out. "Just before the fight started."

Wes Fuller's sire snorted in disgust. "He was busy saving his own neck—skedaddling away from there too fast to see or hear anything! And so blind drunk I dunno how he kept from falling on his face! I ain't real proud to claim him for my kin right now!" Old Man Fuller started to take another swig of his beer, then made an angry grimace and shoved the glass away.

"I hold no brief for that Earp crowd," he said blackly. "A clan of cardsharps and drifters, for my money, that'd do most anything to keep from dirtying their hands earning a living like the rest of us. Maybe it wouldn't have been any great loss if neither side had walked away from that shindig!

"But fair's fair! For every man you talk to that knows for a fact them cowboys was gunned down when all they wanted was to finish their business in town and leave peaceable, you'll find another who'll swear he heard them slanging the Earps and vowing to have it out with them. And which is telling the biggest lies? Who the hell knows! That's why we have a judge to hold hearings. Let *him* sort it out!"

*   *   *

The hearings dragged on. It was well into November before Ike Clanton was at last called to take the stand. The following day, Stockard found Bart Heywood in his study with the *Nugget* spread before him and his face ruddy from anger and excitement. The mine owner struck on the desk and asserted loudly, "So now at last the truth comes out! And by God, it's about time—even if it has to come from a scoundrel like Ike Clanton!"

"Then you think what he's saying is the truth?" Stockard spoke skeptically.

"It's all here, ain't it—for the first time: the real reason Wyatt Earp wanted those three holdup men killed after bungling their stage job back in March. He admitted to Ike it was to shut their mouths so they couldn't never spill it to anybody that Wyatt was the one planned the job and that it was his friend Doc Holliday killed the driver. After they turned up dead, then Ike Clanton was the one that knew too much for his own good!"

"But for what earthly reason would Earp have told him so much? Sounds to me Clanton's talking through his hat, trying to get revenge for his brother and help the sheriff build a case out of nothing."

"But it fits, damn it! Ike has proved the whole purpose of that shoot-out last week was simply to kill him and shut his mouth."

"Nonsense!" Stockard retorted. "If that was so, then why is he the only one who isn't dead? We're to believe they gunned down Tom McLowery while both his hands were in the air, yet when Ike Clanton rushed up to Wyatt Earp and grabbed him by the arm, Wyatt passed up a perfect opportunity to finish him. Instead, he just shook him off and let him run away and hide. So where was the plot to kill him?"

Then, at what he saw in the miner's face, Dan Stockard added quietly, "I guess you don't agree."

"I can't say I do." Heywood turned his head and looked squarely at the other man, and his scowl held a warning of what was coming next. On a tone of heavy reluctance, he continued. "I'll be honest with you. What I do have to say, I'm afraid, is that I'm kind of disappointed in you, Stockard! The reputation you brought with you had me hoping you could do this job, if anybody could—find the evidence I needed to pin that Earp bunch to the wall. Instead, it looks like Ike Clanton has gone and done it for you!"

Stockard returned the look for a long moment. He said finally, "Could this be your way of telling me I've just been fired?"

Heywood lifted a callused hand, then let it fall again. "Looks a little that way, don't it? Unless you come up with something pretty fast, and pretty good. Otherwise, I don't think I can afford you any longer, not for the results you've showed me."

The silence hung while a burning piñon stick popped and settled in the stove. Then, abruptly, Dan Stockard picked up his hat and rose. "If that's how you want it."

This time, when he left, Bart Heywood didn't stand or even say good-bye.

Alone in his room at the Cosmopolitan Hotel, Dan Stockard kicked the door shut on his heel. At a stride, he approached the bed, dragged his suitcase from under it, and undid the clasps, flinging it wide. He opened a drawer of the dresser, took out shirts and underclothing, and carried them to the bed. He paused, ready to fling the garments into the bag. He stood motionless a moment and then, with an angry shake of the head, dropped the clothing onto the bed. He turned and walked to one of the high, narrow windows, where he placed a forearm against the edge of the frame and leaned there, still simmering as he looked blindly down on Allen Street and its lamps burning in the early dusk.

To admit failure and accept dismissal out of hand from an assignment on which he'd gambled his future was something that went savagely against the grain. He was by no means satisfied with what he'd accomplished here in Tombstone, but he was even less satisfied with Bart Heywood's bland assumption that all the answers were in, all questions settled. There was still work needing to be done here, and hardest of all was the thought of quitting with it left hanging in the air.

Yet he couldn't see much to be gained by hanging on, wasting more time and investing his shrinking funds if the man who brought him to this place chose to call him off the job. Better, he supposed, to cut his losses no matter how badly it roweled him even to think of it. . . .

Just then, he heard the furtive rapping of knuckles. Stockard turned from the window and lifted a hand cautiously toward the gap of his coat front as, frowning, he stepped across the room. The knock sounded again, cautious but insistent. He jerked the door wide.

Sid Whelan stood in the opening, and after a glance in either direction along the corridor, he slipped quickly inside. He set his back to the door panel and let it close under the weight of his shoulders. He said hastily, "Don't worry—nobody knows I'm here. I got your room number off the book on the desk."

"What do you want?" Stockard demanded sharply.

Something in his tone caused the man to blink. "Why I came to tell you it's all set. For tomorrow night."

"Oh."

Dan Stockard had actually forgotten the matter that had been tentatively broached between them. Now, at his failure to show any particular enthusiasm, the outlaw's eyes narrowed. "Look here!" he exclaimed. "I've gone and arranged everything. You told me you wanted in; you wouldn't back out on me now?"

"Maybe I've had second thoughts."

"There's a couple hundred in it for you, guaranteed, once the job's done."

Stockard hesitated. A moment ago, he had been impatient to get rid of the man, yet something told him this deserved to be looked into. He said gruffly, "Well—all right. So what's the proposition?"

"We won't go into that now. Be at Contention City tomorrow, about sunset. You'll be met there and given all the details you need to know."

"Just how many others are involved in this?"

"You'll get all that tomorrow."

"I see. . . . ." Stockard left him standing at the door while he turned away and took a small circuit of the musty carpet, frowning as though in debate while Sid Whelan watched him. But this was only for effect, because his mind was already made up. He turned back now, with a shrug and a nod, and told the other man, "If that's how it has to be . . . At sunset, then. You'd better know what you're talking about!"

He closed the door behind his caller and stood deep in thought as footsteps faded down the hallway.

Chapter 15

Stockard had seen Contention City briefly when the stage that brought him to Tombstone stopped to pick up the mail. It was much like Charleston—a huddle of adobes and board shacks dominated by another of the mills that worked the ores from the silver mines of Cochise County. This time, Dan Stockard rode in on a livery-stable animal, at the tail end of a short November day. The sun was already gone behind the rampart of western mountains, and the stir of crisp air along the valley of the San Pedro made him glad of the jacket he carried lashed behind his saddle.

Now that he was here, he had no idea at all what was expected of him. He reined in at a water trough under the droop of a salt cedar. While the rented horse muzzled the scummy water, Stockard looked along the empty street and listened to the voice of the town; a brief twilight settled. Suddenly, he grew alert as a pair of riders swung into view, and he recognized the solid shape of Curly Bill Brocius. The second was the gunman John Ringo. They rode past in a leisurely fashion, apparently without noticing anyone half hidden in the shadows. Stockard let them go by.

For a fact, he hadn't exactly counted on those two when he took Sid Whelan's proposition. Frowning narrowly, he watched them dismount before a Mexican eatery and loop their reins over a crooked hitch rail. As they trooped inside, they were briefly silhouetted against the spill of buttery lamplight from the doorway. The vision left Stockard with sobering second thoughts about what he might have let himself in for.

Shadows deepened, the night breeze stiffened, the last colors leaked out of the sky. And now a single horseman approached. There was still light enough to recognize him, and Stockard touched the livery horse with his heel and eased out of the shadows, speaking Whelan's name. Startled, the outlaw jerked his reins, but then he saw Stockard and eased over to join him.

"I'm a little late," Sid Whelan said gruffly.

Stockard said, "Ringo and Brocius are here."

The outlaw's reaction surprised him. The man seemed alarmed. "Here? In town?" He followed Stockard's nod to where a pair of horses waited in front of the eating shack and swore under his breath. "I didn't figure on that! Let's get out of here before they see us! If they should catch on to what we're up to, Curly Bill will insist on a cut!" Swearing again, he gave his horse a kick, and Stockard fell in beside him.

At least it was clear now that Brocius and Ringo had no part in whatever might be afoot. He was more relieved about that than he cared to admit. Tonight could bring enough danger before it was over without having to think about coming up against *that* pair.

The two riders skirted the eatery. Soon they had left the lights of the town behind as they followed the stage road north into growing darkness. So far, Whelan offered no word of explanation, apparently enjoying making a mystery of things. Stockard held back from asking questions, letting him have things his own way—for now.

Six miles north of Contention, they skirted Drew's Station, where spare animals for the company's stage teams whickered at the scent of passing horses. Shortly afterward, Whelan drew rein, and almost at once the eerie cry of a hoot owl drifted to them from dark scrub growth at the top of a rise ahead. Whelan put his hands to his mouth and produced a fair imitation of the call. This brought an echo, twice repeated. With a grunt of satisfaction, the outlaw lifted the reins and kicked his animal forward. And Dan Stockard, who had already recognized this place, rode after him as the figure of a man stepped into the open and stood waiting for them to come up.

Taking his cue from Whelan, Stockard drew rein and dismounted. The swift night had fallen by now, with a mesh of stars spread thickly overhead. The one who had given the owl-hoot signal spoke now in Jake Flagg's angry voice: "Don't tell me *this* is the one you got for us, Sid! *Him?*" There was naked hostility in the way he peered at the man who had pistol-whipped him on Allen Street, ending his drunken stand against Marshal Earp. "You ain't expecting me to work with this sonofabitch—after what he done to me?"

"All he done," Sid Whelan corrected, "was save your hide from the Earps! Mine, too! Without him stepping in that day, it could've been us filling a hole on Boot Hill right now instead of Billy Clanton and them McLowerys!"

That reminder took Flagg aback, but not by much. "I still don't like him!" he insisted in a sullen tone. "I don't want him in on this job."

"Just what do you intend doing about it?" Dan Stockard challenged, putting toughness into his words.

"He'll do nothing!" Whelan cut in. "Jake, you'll work with him and shut up about it! This one is *my* deal. I set it up, and he's the man I picked. With Frank Stilwell still under suspicion on account of that Bisbee job, we've finally got our chance to get in on some of the *real* action. And I ain't letting anyone back out now!''

There was a tense moment, which ended when Jake Flagg swore under his breath and turned and strode a few paces away. But he didn't answer, and the quarrel appeared to be settled. Whelan turned his attention to his saddle cinch, pulling the latigo tight. Silent minutes crawled by as the night grew older.

Then the trio sighted a double spot of light bobbing and dancing and briefly disappearing again on the dark flats where the ruts of the stage road approached from the south. The lights resolved themselves into the twin side lamps of a coach, heading for Benson after a quick change of teams at Drew's Station.

"Are we supposed to be holding up that stage?" Dan Stockard asked incredulously.

"Naturally. What else?" Sid Whelan countered.

"But I was told this is the identical spot where the job blew up, last March!"

"And for that very reason, it's the last place in the world anyone would expect the same thing to be tried again! The driver and the guard will be remembering how people got killed that other time. I have a hunch it will take the fight out of them."

"Maybe." Stockard didn't argue the point. No sense in raising objections. He'd assumed tonight's operation had to be something on this order. Curiosity had carried him this far; he'd go on playing the cards as they fell.

At an order from Whelan, he mounted again, while Jake Flagg walked into the brush to get the horse he'd tied there. The coach was already near enough that they could hear the muffled thud of hooves and squeak of timbers and see the steady bobbing of the oil lamps burning at either side of the forward boot.

Whelan said, "You'll be wanting this." Stockard saw he was being offered a large square of cloth, of the sort that cowboys hereabout wore around their necks. Though it smelled strongly of sweat, he accepted it and tied it across the lower part of his face in imitation of his companions. Sid Whelan gave his final orders: "I'll start the ball rolling. You two follow my lead. But don't hesitate to let 'em know you're there!"

Jake Flagg, behind his own mask, added a warning for Stockard's benefit: "You better not even *act* like you might slip up, mister! I'll be watching you careful!"

His words—not the threat but the voice that spoke it—drew a sharp look from Stockard. Up to that moment, he could not be quite sure; but now, partly muffled by the cloth, there was no mistaking the voice of the masked bandit who had put a gun on him when he rode the box next to Nat Gower, made him divest himself of his gun, and had even taken his watch and chain. Staring at the man, he suddenly remembered how that business had ended—the swiping blow with the mail sack, the bullet that took Flagg's hat off his head and scattered the holdup attempt. It all must have been humiliating for the leader, and there was no way he would have forgotten. All at once, Stockard thought he had some hint of the real depths of Jake Flagg's dislike of him.

But there was no more time for talk, because the coach was almost on them. With one accord, they split, reining their horses into brush at either side of the road; and Stockard wasn't at all surprised to see Jake Flagg close at his stirrup, keeping an eye on him, just as promised. Ignoring him, Dan Stockard pulled his gun and held it ready as he waited.

The stagecoach took the rise. The creak and slam of timbers, the heavy breathing of the teams, filled the night. The glow of the lamps washed over the crowding brush and showed pale blobs of faces at the windows and the driver and shotgun messenger looming on the forward boot. Dan Stockard caught a glint from the tubes of a shotgun across the knees of the guard. And then he looked at the driver and made out the lean face and drooping yellow mustache of Nat Gower.

Slowed by the pull of gravity, the stage leveled off at the top of the rise. It was then that Sid Whelan's shout came across the darkness. "This here is a holdup! Don't try anything! Driver, stomp that brake and keep both hands in sight!" And Jake Flagg, from the other side, added further warning. "Careful! You're covered from all directions!"

Dan Stockard well knew Nat Gower's uncertain temper and the outrage the man must be feeling. But he was no fool, and with a blistering oath, he hauled in the leathers. The stage bucked to a halt; the horses, held in check, blew and stamped restlessly.

"You, with the shotgun!" Sid Whelan continued in a voice that sounded too loud and too high. "No mistakes, now! Just slide it off your knees—easy! Let it drop!" The guard was in no mood to argue. Stockard thought he must have heard Whelan's nervousness and was experienced enough to know that a bandit with a case of nerves and a gun in his fist could be the most dangerous kind. There was a ringing sound as the shotgun barrels struck a spoke of the big front wheel on its way to the ground, and Whelan said, "Good!"

Now Jake Flagg kneed his animal closer so those inside the coach could see the gleam of his six-shooter. "Don't nobody in there get any ideas, either," he warned. "All I need is one suspicious move and I start shooting. And I won't be too concerned who I hit! You understand?"

They did. If they had heard about a passenger being killed in a holdup here last March, it probably helped keep them quiet. "That's just dandy!" Sid Whelan declared. He suddenly sounded a lot more at ease, even jubilant over the way things were going. "Now! While everybody sits tight, my partner there"—he meant Stockard—"will help you get rid of the thing we come here for. I think you know what I'm talking about, driver. Fetch it up!"

Nat Gower was an unknown quantity. He'd been proud of his record—no successful holdups in all the time since he started handling the reins out of Tombstone. Afraid of what he might do, Stockard gave him no time to think. He kneed his horse forward, saying roughly, "You got your orders! Move!"

After a moment's hesitation, Gower leaned into the boot and, with a grunt, hauled up the treasure chest. "Don't drop it," Stockard said. "Wait till I get a hold." The driver balanced it on the grab-iron. Stockard caught the handle of the box and pulled it over onto his saddle. If the thing had held gold bars, it would have been more than he could handle; silver was heavy enough. "Got it!" he said as he reined back from the coach.

"All right!" Whelan told the driver. "Take this coach out of here. Get going!" And to punctuate the order, he raised his revolver barrel skyward and punched out a couple of shots.

The frightened wheelers tried to climb onto the lead teams. It took an angry yell and quick work by the driver to get them straightened out. In a moment, the stage horses were scrambling into their collars and were off at a headlong run, north toward Benson and the railroad. Another pistol shot sped them on. And as the coach disappeared, Sid Whelan came spurring toward his companion through the dust cloud the vehicle left behind. "Let's go!" He plunged into the brush, and Stockard followed, with Flagg bringing up the rear.

They rode all out. Even though a full white moon was just clearing the mountains to the east, over this terrain and by night it was a risky business; but Stockard knew his companions felt they had to put distance between themselves and the holdup. He set his jaw and dug speed out of the rented horse, hoping he'd drawn a surefooted beast and speculating on what Sid Whelan had next in mind.

It was less than thirty miles to the safety of the Mexican border, but Whelan didn't seem to be thinking of that at all. He held generally to an eastern course and actually began to veer slightly north. Maybe he had a safe hideout prepared or knew a way to lose their trail before an alarm could be raised and a posse took the field. Stockard couldn't begin to guess.

The night deepened. It was going to be a cold one for this desert country, and he thought of the jacket behind his saddle but had no opportunity to get at it. The treasure box seemed to grow heavier, starting to cut off circulation and turn his legs numb. He tried to brace some of its weight against the pommel.

Just as he was beginning to wonder if Whelan meant to run their horses into the ground, the leader pulled rein and, turning, lifted a hand that brought the others to a halt beside him. All three had long since stripped off their masks, and strengthening moonlight showed their faces. "We've been making good time," Whelan said. "I think we better rest our horses."

Wind whipped dry brush and flecked the uneven ground with shadows. Jake Flagg stepped down from the saddle to check his cinch, but the others remained mounted. Watching Stockard shift the balance of the treasure box, Whelan suddenly asked, "That thing getting heavy?"

"It's all right," Stockard said.

"Maybe somebody should spell you."

"I can manage."

He might have spoken too quickly. Something made the other man regard him carefully, for a long moment. Turning to Jake Flagg, who was smoothing down his saddle fender, Sid Whelan said, "Go get it."

The man shrugged and took a step toward Stockard's horse, reaching for the handle of the box. He stopped like that, with arm raised, as he stared into the muzzle of the gun that had slid from under Stockard's coat. "No!" Dan Stockard said it reluctantly. His hand had been forced. Whatever happened, he had no intention of letting this box out of his hands.

He had caught the others completely by surprise. Flagg stood where he had faltered, and Whelan's startled reaction was transmitted through the reins in a way that made his bay horse toss its head and shift its footing. "What is this?" Whelan demanded harshly.

Jake Flagg told him, "I'd say we been tooken in!"

The revolver held, unwavering. As they stared at it, Dan Stockard drew a breath and gave them their answer bluntly. "There's been a change in the program," he said. "I'm keeping the box."

"You bastard!" Flagg's fists knotted. He seemed almost furious enough to charge the drawn gun, but instead he whipped around to vent his anger on Sid Whelan. "This is *your* fault! I told you he wasn't to be trusted, but you had to go and let him play you for a sucker!"

"As for that," Stockard told him, and he was sincere in what he said, "I honestly don't like to use people. Not even crooks like you! It was a case of not having any choice." And Flagg swore at him again from a seemingly bottomless reservoir of hatred.

After his first reaction, Whelan had done and said nothing. He was studying Dan Stockard, as though trying to read his face in the dim moonglow. When he finally spoke, he sounded confident. "Shaw, you've made a bad mistake. That box ain't worth nothing to you."

"That hardly sounds likely. From the heft, it seems as though it would have to be worth quite a lot."

"Not to you," the sandy-haired outlaw repeated. "You don't know how the system operates. I'm telling you straight!" he went on with odd insistence. "The best thing you can possibly do is to give me the box. I'll be willing to forget this happened; I'll even see you get your full share—the two hundred you was promised. But make up your mind, because the way you're headed, you'll get nothing at all!"

Stockard shook his head. "You're wrong about that," he said coolly. "After all, I can always run you both in—and the box, too."

Slowly, Jake Flagg's head came up so that the moon showed his face clearly beneath the brim of his hat. "Run us in?" he echoed. "What the hell! You ain't the *law*."

"Near enough. Actually, a private detective, called in to work on these stage holdups. And it does look like I struck pay dirt!" As they absorbed this, he added, "I'll take your guns. Then we'll head for Tombstone."

He was afraid it wouldn't be that simple. He was ready when, with a furious shout, Jake Flagg whipped the gun out of his belt holster and brought it up, firing.

Stockard had been trying to keep both men covered, a hard-enough job. Now he had to bring his gun to bear on Flagg, who had pivoted as he made his move in order to present a narrower target. Stockard was met by a smear of muzzle flame, blinding at that point-blank distance. The heavy box on his lap received a jolting blow. Flagg's bullet glanced away, but it threw off his shot, and he knew he had missed.

The guns cracked flatly in the night, and Stockard's rented horse nickered in fright and began to act up. Encumbered by the weight across his lap, he was trying to settle it when a new weapon spoke. It came from Sid Whelan, spurring his animal straight at Stockard, who took a stinging blow high on the arm. It drove Stockard off balance—his horse shied, and the next moment he was going out of the saddle, the box falling with him.

A desperate kick freed his foot from the stirrup, saving him from being hung up. Going down, Stockard half turned and landed on hands and belly; the heavy treasure box barely missed landing on top of him. He lay half stunned.

A voice yelled, "You *got* him!"

Another—Sid Whelan's—answered: "Make sure. . . ."

Stockard managed to roll onto his back, not even noticing when his weight came upon the injured arm. Somehow he still had the revolver. He saw Jake Flagg rushing up, a blacker shadow against the night. At the last moment, caution must have induced Flagg to slow, and the gun barrel in his hand glimmered faintly as he raised it.

Dan Stockard fired and knocked Flagg off his feet. As the man fell away, Sid Whelan was revealed charging at Stockard, his horse looming blackly. But Whelan had overridden his enemy. Stars were blotted out as the animal's bulk passed directly overhead—shod hooves thundered, jarring the earth but somehow missing Stockard. Now Whelan reined the bay around and came back, his six-shooter aimed straight downward.

Two guns spoke almost together.

Through the smoke haze, Stockard saw how Sid Whelan was wiped bodily off the saddle. The riderless horse spun aside with loose reins flying, and after that, Dan Stockard lay where he was, gathering his senses, while sounds of violence faded and were replaced by the growing burn of a bullet wound just beginning to thaw.

Chapter 16

The bone wasn't injured, but the muscle of his upper left arm had been painfully scored, and it bled copiously until Stockard finally stanched it with the cloth he had used as a face mask. When he donned his jacket, he let the left sleeve ride empty. Fortunately, the gun-frightened horses had not bolted far. He was able to catch one of them and use it to round up the other pair. His arm was beginning to throb badly now, and it took much of his strength to raise the men he had killed and lay them face down across their saddles. There was no rope to tie them; he had to make do with hooking their belts over the saddle horns. Afterward, he lifted the treasure box onto his own saddle and mounted. Finally, with the lead horses anchored in line by their reins, he was ready to return to Tombstone.

It was a laborious journey. Though his arm had stopped bleeding, the jarring it took, even at a slow walk, was painful. Stockard could feel the blood he'd already lost, and there were times he wondered if he could actually make the half-dozen miles or so he had to cover; but he gritted his teeth and hung on. His gun was reloaded and back in its holster. The night seemed endless, while the moon climbed up the sky. He kept rallying out of a numbing lethargy to the knowledge that tonight's job was only begun.

The moon, a white disc that blanked out the nearest stars, rode high now. Stockard was approaching the outlying houses of Tombstone, sprawled across Goose Flats, when he suddenly became aware of an approaching body of horsemen. Thinking quickly, he drew aside from the wagon road and gained the shelter of a cluster of unlighted buildings. He pulled up barely in time, watching unseen as the cavalcade went by.

He counted a dozen, caught the glint of moonlight on gun metal, and thought he recognized the slim and dapper figure of Sheriff Johnny Behan at their head. Unless he was mistaken, the men beside him were the Wells Fargo investigator, Fred Dodge, and a deputy sheriff named Billy Breakenridge. He needed no explanation. The telegraph wires overhead, on their receding line of poles, had finally brought word from Benson of this latest outrage against a treasure stage, and already the sheriff and a hastily gathered posse were taking the field.

Stockard could have saved them a lot of wasted effort, but he had other plans, and he held where he was, out of sight, while the cavalcade filed past and the night swallowed them. When the dust had drifted and settled, he spoke to his rented horse and came out of the black shadows, the tethered animals following under their swaying and stiffening burdens.

He took a roundabout course through the dark back streets and along Tough Nut, past a lumberyard and rows of darkened miners' cabins and past the dark bulk of a building under construction that he understood would become the courthouse for newly created Cochise County. He had to turn north past the Russ House into Fifth. Nellie Cashman's place was abloom with light, but Stockard rode with head averted and hat drawn low, hoping that the passing of horses with their grim cargo would somehow fail to draw attention or that at least he would not be recognized.

Halfway up the block, an alley stretched behind the cheek-by-jowl buildings that lined Allen Street. Stockard turned into it. There were denser shadows here, but someone had left a lantern burning on a nail beside the rear door of the Wells Fargo office. It shone fully on Stockard and the horses as he drew to a halt, gathering strength to step out of the saddle.

He hadn't yet moved when he heard quick footsteps approaching from behind. He swore and started to draw his gun as he twisted about to see what the danger was—and recognized the last voice he wanted to hear right then, calling his name.

With a groan, Stockard dropped his hand from the holster as Nellie Cashman came into view. She was hatless, a shawl pulled about her against the night wind. "Dan?" she called again. "I thought it had to be you I saw go past. But what in the world—?"

"Get away from here, Nell!" he exclaimed hoarsely. "You don't want any part of this. . . ."

But she came closer, into the lantern glow pooled about the weary clot of horses. That was when she saw what they carried. She stopped dead, and both hands went up to her face in a gesture of horror. Turning to him, she said slowly, "Did you . . . ?"

He nodded heavily. "What does it look like? Yes—I killed them. I had no choice. I've got a job, and I was doing it. You knew it was like this sometimes."

Not looking at her, unutterably weary and low of spirits, Dan Stockard hauled the heavy box off his lap, tried to lower it to the dust, but lost his grip and had to let it thud heavily and topple onto one side. After that, he pulled his leg across the saddle, but when he dismounted there was no strength in his knees, and they buckled under him. He went on down, catching at the stirrup leather to keep from falling on his face.

That caused a gasp to break from Nellie and brought her to him. "Are you all right?"

The momentary weakness had passed, and he was already getting to his feet, waving her away. But she placed an anxious hand on his wounded arm and must have felt the way he flinched away from it. "You're hurt!"

"I'll be all right!" he insisted gruffly. "And I already told you I don't want you here."

"Well, I won't leave!"

It was then that a new voice spoke from the shadows, cutting in on Nellie to say, "For your own good, ma'am, it could be a damned smart idea. . . ."

Stockard's head lifted sharply. For a moment, he could only stare at the one who came toward them into the lantern light—one with the lean shape and wasted features of Doc Holliday. The eyes in Doc's sallow face studied him, then passed for a moment to the woman at his side. Then, as no one spoke, Holliday moved over to the horses. One by one, he lifted the heads of the two dead men, then let them fall back.

He turned to Dan Stockard and said in a cold voice, "Flagg and Whelan . . . Looks like you've had a busy night!" He nodded toward the treasure box on the ground between them. "You fought them for the box?"

"Yes," Stockard said, his tone sharp. "If you want it, you'll have to take it the same way!"

"D'you think I couldn't?"

Their stares met and locked. At that moment, the danger was almost a physical thing between them in the stillness of the alleyway. Nellie must have felt it. She came a step nearer, a hand lifting. "Oh, please!" she begged them both in a broken whisper.

Stockard made an angry gesture. "Move clear of us!"

Then Doc Holliday began to cough. His gaunt shoulders heaved before the first sound came; blindly, he groped for a pocket and brought out a cloth, which he clamped over his mouth. He half turned away, bending nearly double as the rheumy spasm ravaged his lungs. Once begun, he seemed unable to stop, and the others could only stand helplessly by and watch him in his agony, at a loss to do or say a thing.

Finally, with a last shudder, the gunman straightened and settled himself; the handkerchief he shoved into his pocket held a spot of red. Holliday drew a deep and rasping breath. His face, in the lantern light, appeared ghastly as he looked again at the man still waiting for him to take up the challenge.

He shook his head. "Forget it, Stockard," he said harshly. "I'm not interested in a fight. I just wanted to see how you'd act."

Dan Stockard gave a start. "You know my name! You knew all along?"

"Of course—from that time in Texas. I make it my business never to forget a face."

"Yet you never let on you'd so much as laid eyes on me before. . . ."

"It wasn't easy! The night you hit town—in that poker game—you were hell-bent on baiting me for some reason. And I had to sit and swallow it because I was curious as hell to see what a Pinkerton man could be up to."

"I'm not with Pinkerton anymore," Stockard corrected him. "I'm a private operator."

Holliday shrugged. "Small difference. I knew you had *something* in mind, going after me like that."

"It was a gamble I had to take—the quickest way I could think of to make the impression I wanted."

"On trash like this?" Holliday looked with a grimace at the bodies of the dead outlaws. "Well, I see it paid off for you—if this is what you were after!'' He nudged the heavy box with his toe. ''I assume it's the loot from tonight's stage job that sent the sheriff and his posse scooting out of town hell for leather.''

''I notice you didn't go with them.''

''Why should I? I don't owe that bastard Johnny Behan any favors, not after him trying to make me out a stage robber—or get both me and Wyatt strung up for doing in them Clanton and McLowery scum! No, I just stood and watched them go. And then I caught a glimpse of you sneaking into town with this pair of beauties on your towline. I had an idea you'd be heading for the Wells Frago office. I decided to meet you here.''

Stockard glanced toward the closed rear door and lighted windows of the office. ''Who's inside?''

''Marsh Williams, I guess. Or the clerk—hard to say. After the news of another holdup came in on the wire an hour ago, this place was busy as a stepped-on anthill!''

Stockard looked at the box lying between them. ''I suppose I should take this in and put their worries to rest.''

''No doubt it would be appreciated.'' As though it were a casual afterthought, Holliday asked, ''Can I give you a hand?''

Stockard, leaning, felt a sudden rush of light-headedness and a touch of alarm. It was this reminder of his own weakness that made him admit, ''It's a mite unwieldy.''

''And you looked a little peaked,'' Holliday said in a dry tone of voice.

It was only now Stockard realized that, in bending forward, he had let his jacket slide away to reveal the blood-soaked shirt sleeve. Nellie, who had stood silent during all this, exclaimed in an anxious voice, ''You've been *shot*! You shouldn't even be trying to lift that thing. You need a doctor!''

''In good time. When this is taken care of.''

"What about *them*?" Doc Holliday indicated the dead men.

"They won't be going anywhere. They can wait." Legs braced for another try at the heavy box, Stockard paused to frown at the woman. "I told you I don't want you in this. You should be home."

"Without knowing how bad hurt you really are?" She shook her head in stubborn refusal. "You'll not be getting rid of me that easy, Dan Stockard!"

Though he sensed that all danger wasn't over this night, he had to husband his strength, with little to spare for arguing with her Irish stubbornness. Dan Stockard shrugged, and he and Holliday lifted the treasure box between them.

Nellie hurried to open the door as they tramped up the steps and into the express office. Though a couple of lamps were burning, the place seemed empty until Stockard caught a murmur of voices in the partitioned cubbyhole belonging to agent Marshall Williams. He saw the agent and mine owner Bart Heywood seated in there, with Harry Phelps leaning against the wall, wearing his green eye shade and black arm bands.

The talk broke off at the sound of someone in the main room. All three hurried out, wearing looks of astonishment as Stockard and Holliday lifted their burden onto the counter. Marsh Williams, blinking behind his spectacles, found voice to stammer, "What is this?"

"You should know," Stockard answered gruffly. "One of you loaded it for Benson this evening."

"That's not the shipment from my Last Chance mine?" Bart Heywood shoved his way forward to stare at the dusty and battered chest. "How the hell did *you*—?" And then he caught sight of Doc Holliday, and his face darkened with quick suspicion.

Stockard set him straight with a shake of the head.

"Don't look at Holliday. All he had to do with it was to give me a hand toting the thing inside. It was getting kind of heavy!"

"Sure, and it's no wonder!" Nellie Cashman cried. She placed a hand on Stockard's arm as she told the rest, "Can't you see the man has been *shot*? He shouldn't even be standing here talking to you!"

"It's all right, Nell," he assured her quietly. "I think I can hold out until this business is settled." And there was something in his look that told her she was not to interfere. Biting her lip, Nellie dropped her hand and drew back, her concern for him etched in her troubled frown.

Heywood, for his part, could not keep his eyes from the recovered treasure box. He said now, harshly, "Open it, somebody. I want to see for myself."

"I'll fetch the key," Harry Phelps said quickly, and started for his desk.

But Marshall Williams had different ideas. "The lock is intact," he pointed out. "There's no sign it's been tampered with at all. We'll leave it as it is."

Dan Stockard, on braced legs, felt the floor starting to take on an alarming slant. One hand caught the edge of the counter, tightening there to steady him. His voice was firm enough as he pointed out, "I've been to a lot of trouble fetching this. If it's all the same, I'd like to see the owner satisfied. And after that I want a receipt!"

"I go with that!" the miner agreed quickly. "Go ahead— open it!"

Harry Phelps hesitated, the key in his hand. Williams, scowling with his mouth drawn tight, shook his head. But the other two were adamant, and the clerk, reading the odds, must have seen no choice. He made his decision and fumbled the key into the lock. It sprang open, and he lifted the lid on the contents of the battered chest.

For a moment, staring, no one spoke. It was Heywood who exclaimed hoarsely, "It's *lead*! Lead bars!" He reached and pawed at the topmost layer, exposing more beneath. He picked up one of the bars, weighed it in his hand, and angrily threw it back. *"Where the hell is my silver?"*

Marsh Williams had found his voice. "It's obvious, isn't it? There's been a switch!" He looked up, and his eyes, gone hard behind the wire-rimmed lenses, sought Dan Stockard's. "Shaw, just what do you think you're trying to get away with?"

"There's been a switch, all right," Stockard said. "But not my doing."

Heywood hurried to back him up. "He's right! Before we start throwing accusations," the miner pointed out, "there's something you ought to know, Marsh: This man's name is really Stockard. He's a detective I hired to look into these bullion holdups. I don't know what any of this means, but it begins to look like he's found something!"

Dan Stockard couldn't give the two Wells Fargo men long for the news to sink in; in truth, he didn't know for certain how much time he still had. "The job's not quite finished yet," he said bleakly. He turned to the clerk. "Harry! What do you know about this?"

The clerk blinked at the hard tone of his voice. "Me?" he stammered. "Nothing!"

"You real sure?" Stockard threw it at him, temper shortened by an alarming increase in weakness and pain. "A man who figures he's too big for the job he's stuck in—who works off his frustrations taking bigger risks than he can afford at the faro tables? You absolutely certain you haven't been trying to hit back at Wells Fargo and get even with the world?"

The clerk's face had turned blotchy. His voice shook.

"Damn you! I've never touched a dime that didn't belong to me!"

Any doubts that Stockard had been harboring about Harry Phelps faded before the honest fury he read in that statement. It was a half-formed suspicion he had been holding for some time, and it died hard. "But you see, don't you," he said as stern as ever, "that leaves us only one other suspect." The six-shooter slid from its holster, and he pointed it at the Wells Fargo agent. "Williams," he demanded, "just what is it you keep in the safe in your private office?"

The man blinked, but he recovered quickly. "Nothing!" he snapped indignantly. "Nothing that's anybody's damn business! And take that gun off me!"

"Not yet," Stockard answered. "How about opening that safe first and letting us have a look for ourselves?"

Bart Heywood was staring from one to the other in bewilderment and alarm. "Come on now, Stockard!" he protested. "Ain't you getting out of your depth?"

"No," Dan Stockard replied, not taking his eyes from the one he was accusing. "But I think Marsh Williams is! A boxload of silver ingots has disappeared tonight. They've got to be somewhere—and if he did stash them in his office, he can hardly have had a chance to move them. . . . All you have to do to prove me wrong," he reminded the agent, "is to open the safe and show us."

Heywood had grown a shade more thoughtful, less sure in his indignation. He gave the Wells Fargo man an uncertain look. "What do you say, Marsh? It'll shut him up," he pointed out.

"No!" Williams shouted it. "Damned if I do any such thing. I don't have to! That safe is my personal property."

"You're mistaken," Stockard reminded him. "It's the property of Wells Fargo!" He turned to the clerk. "Do you have the combination?"

Harry Phelps was wide-eyed, stunned at what was being suggested. He shook his head. "Marsh never gave it to me." He hesitated before he added, blurting it out, "But I do know he has it written down in a notebook—in his coat pocket."

"Oh?" Stockard said, turning back to the Wells Fargo agent. "Looks like it's up to you, then, Williams. You have a choice. Do you hand it over, or do we have to take it off you?"

For a moment, they stood unmoving, deadlocked in a clash of wills. All at once, a sheen of sweat burst out along the man's receding hairline; the eyes behind the lenses glittered. Doc Holliday, who had stood by without speaking during all this, exclaimed suddenly, "Don't trust him, Stockard! I never have. I think you're dealing with a snake. . . ."

Stockard didn't need the warning. He waited while Williams flicked a hot glance at Holliday and back again. The agent's chest swelled on an indrawn breath. "All right," Williams said, and he started a hand toward the inner pocket of his coat.

"Wait!" Batting the hand aside, Stockard reached into the pocket himself. What he found was not a book but a stubby, twin-barreled pocket derringer. He brought it out and shook his head reprovingly as he heard, behind him, Bart Heywood's exclamation—if Heywood still had any belief in the man, it must have faded quickly.

Dan Stockard put the derringer on the counter, and this time his cold look knocked further resistance out of Williams. At a terse command, the Wells Fargo agent lifted his arms while Stockard searched him and almost instantly found what he wanted.

Not taking his eyes from Williams, he tossed a small, leather-bound book to Harry Phelps, who caught it and fumbled through the pages. "Here it is."

"Use it!"

"I want to see this!" Bart Heywood exclaimed, his suspicions fully roused by this time. While the others held where they were, he followed the clerk into the cubbyhole office. In the waiting stillness, Phelps, referring to the book, began to work the dial of the big safe. Stockard, still holding his own against the throb of his wounded arm, kept his gun and his eye on the Wells Fargo agent, whose face had become unreadable except for the twitching of a muscle in one clean-shaven cheek.

Suddenly, the clerk stepped back; the heavy door swung open. With an exclamation, Heywood shoved him out of the way, and they could all see, stacked neatly, a gleam of silver ingots. For a moment, no one spoke. Then Harry Phelps turned a horrified face to the mine owner. "The man was right! It's your shipment," he stammered. "But—by God, I swear *I* know nothing about this!" He was trembling as he came, almost running, to confront the group in the main room, looking like a man who had received the shock of his life. He turned to Stockard. "You've got to believe me!" Whatever's been going on—I had no part in it!"

"Of course you didn't," Dan Stockard said. "It was Marshall Williams's private setup. Unless he can be forced to tell or has kept records of some kind, Wells Fargo may never know how much bullion he got away with or how it was disposed of."

All eyes turned on the agent, whose face had become a pale and unreadable mask. And Stockard continued: "He had to plan carefully. There was always the risk that a holdup would fail—a guard might prove too zealous or something else might go wrong. A box showing up at its destination filled with lead bars would have been damned hard to explain! But he took the chance, and apparently it never happened."

"Wait a minute!" Bart Heywood had followed Harry

Phelps back into the main room. "It must have happened last March! They killed a couple of people, but they never stopped the stage."

"That was amateurs. Bill Leonard and his friends were working on their own. No, you can believe that any jobs Williams involved himself in would have been planned better than that!"

"But all this substituting of lead bars—was it actually necessary? If his own men were to do the stealing . . ."

Dan Stockard said patiently, "Isn't it obvious? Once those outlaws actually laid hands on a box of real silver, do you suppose Williams would ever have seen it again? They'd have been across the border with it and clean gone from this country! No, he arranged for them to pick up something absolutely worthless so that they had to turn it back to him if they wanted to get paid. His going price was two hundred per man."

During all this, Marshall Williams had stood silent, listening to the charges against him. Now he found his voice. "All lies!" he exclaimed angrily. "Every word of it! Certainly I made that switch today, but it was only because I'd had warning someone intended to make a try for the shipment— and my information turned out to be right! For all your talk, there's no way you can make anything more than that out of it or pin any sort of crime on me. You haven't a shred of proof!"

He was right, of course. Stockard's whole case was built on supposition, and a man as shrewd as Marsh Williams could turn the evidence around to mean whatever he wanted it to. Alarmingly, at that moment Stockard felt near the end of his strength. The gun in his hand was a heavy weight, and he wasn't sure how long he could keep a tight grip on his senses.

But he had one bluff left in him, and he played it. "You're wrong. I've got proof. There's a couple of men tied up out in the alley. Their names are Whelan and Flagg. All they have to do is tell their story. . . .''

The blow, when it came, was without warning. Williams's fist struck his wounded arm a solid blow. Pain lanced through him. He felt his fingers open, unable to retain their hold on the gun, and his knees gave way. He fell heavily and heard Nellie Cashman's cry of alarm as the light splintered into pulsing blackness.

Chapter 17

Dan Stockard didn't completely lose consciousness. He felt hands that he sensed were Nellie's, but they were pulled instantly away. There was a noise of scuffling; then, gradually, his head cleared, and he found himself on the floor. Somewhere a voice was speaking, one that sounded like Marshall Williams's, but distorted with some powerful emotion. Stockard heard it say, "I'm warning you! You'd all better stay back if you don't want me to use this. . . ."

Dan Stockard forced his head up, and at what he saw he almost thought the blood in his veins had turned to ice. Williams had retrieved the derringer that Stockard had laid on the counter. And what was far worse, he evidently had managed to cut Nellie Cashman off as she rushed to Stockard's aid. Now, with an arm clamped about her waist, he was holding her pressed against him like a shield. The gun's double barrels were pressed firmly against the side of her head.

It had been enough to stop Nellie from struggling. She stood utterly motionless, anxious to do nothing to antagonize him; there was stark terror in her eyes, and her face lost all its color. The others in the room had also reacted by freezing in their places. Bart Heywood stammered, "My God, man! You wouldn't!"

"I will if you don't stay back! Don't crowd me. I could never stand for anyone to crowd me!"

Dan Stockard tried desperately to speak, but his throat seemed to be locked tight. But now there was a sound from Doc Holliday. The gambler had been caught, like everyone else, by the sudden threat to Nellie Cashman. As he saw the little gun at her temple, his own long-barreled Colt, already half drawn, slid back into its holster. Nevertheless, there was something quietly menacing in his wasted features as he demanded suddenly, "Was Wyatt Earp crowding you, Marsh? Would that have been the reason you tried to sic Ike Clanton on him?"

That brought the man's head whipping around. And though Holliday got no more answer than a scowl, he seemed satisfied with what he read in it. "I couldn't help but wonder," Doc said, nodding bleakly, "whether you were really drunk or only faking that night you shot off your mouth to Ike about his deal with Wyatt. Now I'm wondering if you might have thought Wyatt was coming too close to figuring out how you'd been piping off these bullion shipments—so you deliberately planted a notion with Ike, hoping it would lead to him and McLowery killing Wyatt and getting rid of him for you.

"Is that what you tried to do, Marsh?"

Williams glared at him, his mouth working, but he neither confirmed nor denied Holliday's guess. Instead, he told the room, "I want all of you to stay just as you are. Don't even move! The lady and I are going out that door yonder."

He seemed to have forgotten all about the cache of silver in his office safe; his thoughts were focused solely on escape. He gave Nellie a nudge forward, and with that gun threatening her, her eyes looked enormous against the pallor in her cheeks as she obeyed, very nearly stumbling. Like the others, Stockard could do no more than watch helplessly.

After the first few steps, Williams made a fast pivot, dragging his hostage around with him; thus, he could still keep an eye on the room as they continued to move, backing up now, the remaining distance to the door. There he paused to give a final warning. "If you want to see her again, alive, you won't try to follow us! You won't move out of this room for the next ten minutes. I hope that's clear!"

No one answered. Williams shouldered open the door, which had been left ajar when Stockard and Holliday entered with the treasure box. He quickly swung the woman through and jerked the panel shut behind him.

Immediately, Doc Holliday swore and started forward, pulling his gun. Stockard found his voice. "No! He meant it! He's desperate enough to kill her—you saw his face when he was talking about being crowded!"

Scowling, the gunman halted. And now Stockard, under the spur of necessity, found strength to haul himself to his feet. He saw his gun, where it had fallen from his hand, and picked it up. He swayed a little as he looked around at the others; in that moment, there was a spurt of hoofbeats in the alley behind the office as a horse took off at a run.

The sound quickly faded. Stockard was already hurrying for the door, with Holliday close behind him.

They burst into the alley to find the lantern still burning, its light showing two horses standing patiently, the bodies of the outlaws still jackknifed across their saddles. But the animal Stockard had hired from the O.K. Corral was gone. He saw Nellie then, a crumpled heap beside the steps. Everything else forgotten, Stockard got to her and knelt, gently and fearfully raising her. With a great rush of relief, he saw her open her eyes—eyes that were dazed for a moment but instantly cleared as she recognized him. "Dan!"

"Are you hurt?"

She pushed a hand uncertainly through the tangle of her

brown hair. "Not really. He shoved me aside off the steps. I think I hit my head. . . ." Suddenly, her expression filled with concern. "But—*you*?"

"I'm all right," he said roughly, determined that she must not know he was going on nerve alone. His attention was taken then by Doc Holliday. Having seen at a glance that Marshall Williams was gone and Stockard's rented horse with him, Holliday went hurriedly to one of the other animals. It was Sid Whelan's bay. He jerked Whelan's belt free of the saddle horn and unceremoniously dumped the outlaw's stiffening body. After that, he cursed the skittish horse to stand still while he gathered the reins, stabbed a toe into the stirrup, and heaved his wasted frame into the leather.

By then, Dan Stockard had reached him on uncertain legs. "Doc!" he cried. "You're not going after him!"

"I know *you're* not!" the gunman shouted from the saddle with reins lifted, the bay restive under him. Looking down at the wounded man, he said scornfully, "Hell! You can hardly stay on your feet!"

Stockard tried to grab the bridle but missed as the horse swung its head beyond his reach. "Damn it, he isn't yours! The law, and Wells Fargo—it's *their* place to deal with him."

The wasted features of the consumptive took on an ugly cast in the lantern light. "The *hell* with the law and Wells Fargo! That sonofabitch tried to set up Wyatt Earp for killing—he never denied it! And nobody does that to a friend of John Holliday's!"

The iron in his tone warned Stockard. There was no arguing with this strange man's notions of friendship, whether it meant borrowing Wyatt Earp's disguises without permission for a friend to use in a projected holdup or going after the one whose betrayal of Wyatt had led to the gunfight near the O.K. Corral. Knowing he lacked the strength to stop him,

Dan Stockard lowered his arm and stepped back. Holliday jerked the bay around and sent it off down the alley, shod hooves spraying loose dirt and gravel.

Just then, Bart Heywood came cautiously out of the Wells Fargo building in time to catch Dan Stockard as he fell.

The check, written in Bart Heywood's own hand and over Heywood's rough signature, was gratifyingly large. There had been no quibbling over Stockard's itemized list of expenses, and on his own the miner had added a considerable bonus. "Something extra," he explained as he tore the check from the book and handed it over. "For a job well done! What are your plans now?" he added.

"I'm not sure," Stockard answered as he placed the check in his pocket. "Heading back for San Francisco, I suppose, and looking for another assignment."

"The reason I ask is I took the liberty of recommending you to some people I know over in New Mexico who are having some trouble that could use a detective of your caliber— some high-grading going on at one of the mines at Silver City. The owners are anxious to track down the ones that are leaving their shifts with their pockets full of ore. Sounds to me like something right down your alley. Anyway, I got this telegram back less than an hour ago." He handed it across the desk. "They need someone fast, and what's more, they should pay well for results. The job's waiting if you want to get over there and check it out."

"I surely will!" Dan Stockard exclaimed. "As quick as I can make it—and thank you!"

The miner shrugged meaty shoulders. "The least I could do, especially after the bad time I'm afraid I gave you. You certainly delivered! Exposing Williams for us was more than we had a right to expect from any one man. The rest is up to us.''

Fred Dodge—present at this final meeting in his true role of a Wells Fargo operative instead of a faro dealer—made a grudging admission. ''Your methods had mine beat,'' he told Dan Stockard. ''I came to have some suspicions, but once I'd made the mistake of taking Williams into my confidence because he was a company man, I lost any real chance I would ever have had of catching up with him.''

Stockard remembered that remark as he stood late that afternoon by the window of his hotel room, looking again at the telegram and thinking of what it could mean toward establishing himself in the line of work he'd chosen.

Personally, he was strongly of the opinion the world would never catch up with Marsh Williams. In almost two weeks since the night he disappeared, no one seemed to have a clue as to what had happened to him. Doc Holliday, after a couple of days' mysterious absence, unobtrusively resumed his usual haunts—the gaming tables of the various saloons and gambling halls he favored. But if, indeed, he knew the fate of the vanished Wells Fargo agent, he never dropped a hint; any mention of the man in Holliday's presence received a stony glare that promptly led to a change of subject.

Dan Stockard drew his own conclusions. They didn't include the likelihood that the missing man would ever be seen again . . . by anyone.

He returned the telegram to his coat pocket. A glance at his watch said it was time to go. His bill at the desk was paid, and he felt affluent enough to give a youngster a dollar to run his luggage down the street to the Wells Fargo office, where the stage would pick it up. All that remained to be done here was put on his hat and close the door of the room behind him.

Newly mended tissues were still sore, and he half consciously favored them as he emerged upon Allen Street. Dr.

Goodfellow had wanted him to give himself more time to mend, but Stockard was a restless man, and he had already grown impatient with enforced idleness. And the job offer in that telegram was an opportunity he knew he had to follow up.

The winter day was crisp and invigorating, if not really cold, and distant mountains held a scurf of snow. Experiencing only a little discomfort from stretching muscles, Stockard walked to the corner of Fifth Street and was about to cross to the south side of Allen Street when he noticed the pair of men in front of the Oriental Saloon on the northeast corner. He changed his course to go over to join them, and Wyatt and Virgil Earp watched him approach. Wyatt failed to return his nod of greeting or show any change of expression when Stockard told him, "I want to congratulate you on the outcome of the hearing."

The gray eyes met his stonily. "Thanks."

"I read your testimony, in the *Nugget,*" he went on. "A good job. You made a liar of Ike Clanton at every point. After you were through, there could hardly have been much question about the verdict."

It was Virgil who said, "Judge Spicer decided entirely in our favor. He ruled we were performing an official duty in trying to disarm men who were threatening the peace of the community, and had every right to defend ourselves. He gave us everything we could have asked for."

Not quite everything, Stockard thought.

He understood that in giving his dismissal of the murder charge, the judge had first reprimanded Marshal Earp. According to Spicer, it had been poor judgment to deputize members of his own family for a confrontation with the Clantons and McLowerys—men well known to have been their personal enemies. Stockard glanced at the front of Virgil's coat. Having been cleared of all charges, he was again wearing his marshal's badge. But seven men had already announced they would seek his office in the upcoming January election, and it was unlikely Virgil could retain the only official post any of the Earps held.

Nothing had been settled, Stockard realized. There were rumors of threats against the Earps, against Judge Spicer and Mayor Clum. He could see nothing but continuing violence for this town of Tombstone.

"That injured leg of yours seems all right again," he commented.

"I get around," Virgil Earp said briefly.

And then Wyatt, who had been eyeing Stockard with cold dislike, threw a challenge that showed what was on his mind. "So the reason you came here was to pin a stage holdup on me!"

"If you'd been guilty, I'd have had to try. I'm just as pleased it didn't work out that way."

"And your name's really Stockard. . . . Or *is* it?" Wyatt added with chill skepticism.

"It is. Holliday knew all the time. I'm surprised he never told you."

"Not the first secret he's kept from me!" Wyatt said sharply, and Dan Stockard knew he was thinking of a handful of homemade disguises, lent without his permission, that could have incriminated him in a botched holdup of which he'd known nothing at all.

A strange man, this Wyatt Earp—a paradox of a man in Stockard's final judgment. Physically brave, yet a braggart. No doubt reasonably honest, but cold by nature and cruel to his women. Shrewd and yet at the same time naive enough to think he could make a deal with a personal enemy like Ike Clanton and never have it come to light. Naive enough, too, not to realize when he was being used by the owners of the town, powerful men who wouldn't hesitate to be rid of him once they saw him as a liability. . . .

Abruptly, Wyatt Earp turned and stalked away into the Oriental. Virgil, seeing Stockard's expression as he watched the man go, said suddenly, "You got to understand about Wyatt. The Earps have been a wandering clan, looking for the big break and never finding it. Wyatt brought us here to Tombstone two years ago, thinking sure this was the place where we all could make a place for ourselves and find what we always been looking for. It begins to look now as though his big dream has come unstuck, and he's finding it hard to take. So are the rest of us." Then, abruptly changing the subject, he said, "I hear you're leaving town."

"This evening. On the Benson stage."

Virgil Earp put out his hand. "Have a good trip. Don't get yourself held up," he added. His slight smile, as they shook hands, was the first hint of friendliness Dan Stockard remembered having seen in any of this dour and dangerous family. . . .

A brief stop at the Wells Fargo office confirmed that his belongings had been delivered and would be stowed aboard when the evening stage pulled up to take on freight and passengers. For a moment, he watched Harry Phelps at work, no longer wearing the green eye shade of a clerk but busily managing the whole operation as he filled in for the missing Marshall Williams. Stockard understood it was likely Phelps would get the nod to take over the agent's job permanently, there being no one else better qualified or with as complete knowledge of the workings of the office. It was the job he had always wanted. Stockard hoped it would take the edge off his habitual discontent and keep him too busy to have any time for the faro tables. Things appeared to have taken a better turn for Harry Phelps.

There was one final call that had to be made—the most important of all.

When he entered the lobby of the Russ House, it was empty except for Nellie Cashman, standing behind the desk and making penciled notations in a record book. Her head was bent above her work, and she seemed unaware someone had entered. Yet he had a sure feeling she knew very well when he came and stood a moment, silently observing her— the dainty shape of her shoulders, the sheen of dark curls combed neatly in place.

"Nell," he said.

Even then she did not immediately look at him, though the pencil went still in fingers that all at once began to tremble slightly. She laid it down and closed the book and only then lifted her dark eyes to his. Her face was very pale.

"You've come to say good-bye, haven't you?"

He could only stare. "But—how—?"

"How did I know? I just had a feeling."

Stockard studied her expression, trying to read the emotion reflected there, wondering if the shine in her lovely eyes was of unshed tears. "I *do* have to go," he admitted. "If I hurry, I've got a job waiting in New Mexico. But, Nell, I don't want this to be good-bye! It's up to you. . . ." He took a breath. "I've put off asking you this because I couldn't be sure what your answer would be. Now, suddenly, it's almost too late. I'm asking you to go with me. I know you can't right now, but maybe you could join me later, after you've had time to wind things up here. . . ."

She was staring at him. "Dan—are you saying you want me to—?"

"I'm asking you to marry me!" But as he said the words and failed to find in her expression what he had been hoping for, he knew what her answer would be.

Her glance fell away, her eyes filling with tears. "I wish

it could be . . . but it can't.'' When her gaze lifted again to his, she spoke with an intensity that was freighted with emotion. "Dan, listen to me—please! I can't help being what I am, and neither can you. I've been independent too long. I can't give up the life I've known or the work I've chosen and settle down to keeping house in San Francisco or some other town, always waiting—or only hoping—for my husband to come safely home to me!

"Nor can I ask you to give up a career you've trained and worked for just because you know it's one I don't like very much! I'd always be worrying, always wondering what kind of danger you might be in. Maybe in time I'd even get in the way and risk both our lives again, as I did that night in the Wells Fargo office! I'd be so concerned about you, every minute of the time, that it would make me a hindrance and not a help to you. It would never work, Dan. You know it wouldn't.''

"It might," he protested weakly.

Yet even as he spoke, he knew with a heavy certainty that she was right. She had the strength and the courage to recognize and face up to the truth. And after all, it was her strength and courage that had first attracted him and taught him to love her. He drew a breath.

"What I know," he said slowly, "is that you're different from any woman I've ever met, and I'll never be able to forget you. But I'm going to try like hell!''

"When will you be leaving?" she asked after a moment.

"In just about fifteen minutes.''

"Dan . . .'' Her hand groped toward him across the desk. He caught it, and their fingers clasped in desperate intensity. Stockard leaned toward her, his gaze pinned upon her soft mouth. At that instant, however, other people walked into the room, talking loudly. Reluctantly, he drew back; for a moment longer, they gazed at one another, oblivious of everything around them.

"Good-bye, Nell," Stockard said then, and with a final squeeze, he dropped her hand.

"Good-bye—my dear." She spoke so softly, he didn't hear the words but read them on her lips. He knew she was watching when he turned and walked away from her, out onto the dark, windswept streets of Tombstone.

Epilogue:
What Happened After

A few of the characters in this story—Dan Stockard, Bart Heywood, Harry Phelps, Sid Whelan, Jake Flagg, Nat Gower— are fictitious. Most of the others are real, and some of them had interesting later histories.

For the Earps, big trouble had only begun. Later that year, on December 28, 1881, Virgil Earp was ambushed on the street by parties unknown, and his left arm was permanently crippled. The following March, someone opened up on Morgan Earp through a window of Hatch's Billiard Parlor and killed him. This was the end for the family in Tombstone. It was decided that Morgan's body, the crippled Virgil, and their wives should all be sent to Colton, California, where the parents of the Earps were living.

Wyatt and a bodyguard of his friends escorted the wagon to the railroad at Benson, put the party on the train, and stayed with them as far as Tucson. In the train yard there, they ran into Frank Stilwell, the stage-robbing deputy sheriff with a predilection for *sugar,* who Wyatt believed had had a part in the killing of his brother Morgan. Stilwell's body was found later, filled with lead, and a murder warrant was issued on Wyatt.

The warrant was never served. In Tombstone to collect a few belongings, Wyatt simply turned his back when Sheriff Behan tried to arrest him, and left town, never to return. With Doc Holliday and others, he went on a hunt for those he considered his brothers' attackers. Among those he claimed to have found and killed was Curly Bill Brocius himself, though no one ever produced the body.

Soon Wyatt left Arizona and spent the rest of his life as a wanderer, together with Sadie Marcus, who soon joined him and later became his third wife, Mattie being the second. He followed the gold strikes and operated saloons in the Yukon, in Alaska, and at Tonopah, Nevada, among other places. His last years he prospected in California, and he died in near poverty in Los Angeles in 1929.

Mattie, abandoned and left destitute by Wyatt, spent a year at Kate Holliday's boardinghouse in Globe before ending up at Pinal, Arizona, where she fell into prostitution and finally, in 1888, took her own life with an overdose of laudanum. Her miserable fate is one of the blackest marks to be charged against Wyatt Berry Strapp Earp.

Virgil Earp, like all of that clan, was also a wanderer—it was a habit inherited from the old man, Nicholas, who had been constantly on the move, pulling up stakes and shuttling back and forth between Missouri and California. Virgil was elected for a term as marshal of Colton, California, but all the rest of his life he never stayed anywhere very long. He died of pneumonia in 1906 in Goldfield, Nevada—still another mining camp.

Doc Holliday went to Colorado for a few last, restless years, until consumption finished him off in 1887. He and Wyatt had parted company by then—very likely because of Wyatt's suitcase of disguises and Doc's connection with the Benson stage holdup. But to the last, Doc remained a loyal champion of the man who had been his friend.

Kate Holliday (who had been born Mary Katherine Haroney) remained loyal to Doc and was near him when he died. A year later, she married a blacksmith named Cummins, but eventually walked out on him. She died in 1940 in the Arizona Pioneers' Home.

Johnny Behan's later career was not distinguished. He lost his bid for election to the sheriff's office he'd been holding by appointment and spent the rest of his life as a political hack. He moved from one appointed job to another, as far afield as China and Buffalo, New York, with a few months sandwiched in as assistant superintendent of the Arizona prison at Yuma. But he was an alcoholic, and none of his jobs ever lasted long. He died in 1901 at Tucson.

Shortly after the O.K. Corral gunfight, Marshall Williams disappeared from Tombstone under strange circumstances and was never heard of again. Fred Dodge, the Wells Fargo detective, said later he was convinced Williams had been involved in the theft of bullion shipments; he was equally certain of Wyatt Earp's innocence. Dodge was to serve, incidentally, as a pallbearer at Wyatt's funeral.

Mystery also surrounds the death of John Ringo (or Ringgold). In July 1882, he was found sitting with a bullet in his head under a black oak clump not many miles from Tombstone. If it was murder and not suicide, no one has ever proved who killed him, though the honor has long been claimed for Wyatt Earp.

Ike Clanton, whose loud mouth was the main cause of the famous gunfight that killed his brother and the McLowerys, fled to Mexico to escape the Earps. After they left Arizona, he returned and picked up his rustling where he'd left off. A sheriff finished him off in 1887.

Alvira Earp—Virgil's feisty little Allie—outlived them all. At the time she died, in 1947, she was one hundred years old and high-spirited to the last.

Finally, there was Nellie Cashman, the "miners' angel" whose boardinghouse still stands in Tombstone. Nellie never married. This extraordinary woman, devoutly religious, known for her Irish beauty and her concern for the sick and the homeless, continued to act as an angel of mercy in one mining camp after another. In boots and jeans, she worked prospecting claims of her own. She followed the great gold rush to the Yukon and ended her years in Canada the way she had always lived them. She died, a legend, in 1925.

And as for the "town too tough to die," Tombstone still clings to life, its boom-town days ended when the mines, drowned out by flooding at the lower levels, finally closed in 1910. But today those memories are alive—among the richest in the living romance of the American West. . . .

★ WAGONS WEST ★

A series of unforgettable books that trace the lives of a dauntless band of pioneering men, women, and children as they brave the hazards of an untamed land in their trek across America. This legendary caravan of people forge a new link in the wilderness. They are Americans from the North and the South, alongside immigrants, Blacks, and Indians, who wage fierce daily battles for survival on this uncompromising journey—each to their private destinies as they fulfill their greatest dreams.

☐	24408	**INDEPENDENCE!**	**$3.95**
☐	22784	**NEBRASKA!**	**$3.50**
☐	24229	**WYOMING!**	**$3.95**
☐	24088	**OREGON!**	**$3.95**
☐	23168	**TEXAS!**	**$3.50**
☐	23381	**CALIFORNIA!**	**$3.50**
☐	23405	**COLORADO!**	**$3.50**
☐	20174	**NEVADA!**	**$3.50**
☐	20919	**WASHINGTON!**	**$3.50**
☐	22925	**MONTANA!**	**$3.95**
☐	23572	**DAKOTA!**	**$3.95**
☐	23921	**UTAH!**	**$3.95**

Now Available!
The Complete Sackett Family Saga in a Boxed Set

THE SACKETT NOVELS OF LOUIS L'AMOUR

$39.95   (01379-3)

Now, for the first time, the 16 novels of the Sackett family have been collected in four handsome large-size volumes with a beautifully designed gift box. Each volume has a special introduction by L'Amour.

These best-selling L'Amour novels tell the story of the American frontier as seen through the eyes of one bold family, the Sacketts. From generation to generation, the Sacketts conquered the frontier from the wild forests of the East to the dust cattle trails of the Great Plains to the far mountains of the West. Tough and proud, the Sacketts explored the wilderness, settled the towns, established the laws, building a mighty Western tradition of strength and courage.

You can enjoy all these exciting frontier stories of the Sacketts by ordering your boxed set today. And remember, this boxed set is the perfect gift for a L'Amour fan.